Praise for Stephen H. Foreman's

Home: A Love Story

"In *HOME: A LOVE STORY*, Stephen Foreman uses his gift of incisive and poetic language to capture the breadth and depth of humanity, relationships, a deep understanding of nature, and the inevitable passage of time that shapes us all. It is a profound work of heartbreak, humor, wonder, sorrow and, above all, love. It is his finest novel." **—Eric Rickstad, author of *LILITH***

"What a warm-hearted gift this story is! Reuben Henry is an American hero of the classic—meaning, the very best—kind. Brave and cunning in battle, sensitive and compassionate towards others, even to those who stick in his craw. If there were a million more like him, we would live in a better country. For now, it's enough to have him contained and evoked between covers in this funny, moving mountain reverie. You may also learn at least a couple of things that could save your life—or save you some trouble." **—Gene Seymour, contributor to *CNN Opinion, The Nation, The Washington Post*, and *The Baffler***

"A beautiful love note to the Catskills, and to life. Wise and witty, hard-earned and heartfelt." **—Jon Scieszka, National Ambassador for Young People's Literature**

"Through the eyes of Thea, we meet Reuben Henry, aka Poppa, the man who has lovingly raised her from infancy. Poppa is a true American original, a blend of seeming contradictions: educated and homespun; a proud Marine and a seeker of social justice. In late night talks over salami and ginger ale, or hunting turkey and deer, Poppy tells stories to Thea—of his brilliant wife who died too soon, of his hardscrabble childhood in West Virginia, of his global travels as a civil engineer, of his delicious revenge on bigoted neighbor Dub Tuttle. Readers will fall under Poppy's spell just as Thea has, and miss him terribly when they finish this original, funny, entertaining book."   **—Jenny Allen,** *The New York Times, Esquire, Good Housekeeping*

"If you like prime, satisfying writing—sharp-edged stories full of finely-tuned sentences; if you like to be surprised by choices of words and fresh, clever phrases, if you like to be impressed by a writer's breadth of experience and knowledge, *Home: A Love Story*, should quite oblige you, more and more as the pages fly by."   **—Bob Getz, retired award-winning columnist,** *Wichita Eagle*

ALSO BY STEPHEN H. FOREMAN

Watching Gideon

Toehold

Journey

HOME: A LOVE STORY

Alternative Book Press.

alternativebookpress.com

Copyright © 2025 Stephen H. Foreman

All Rights Reserved. First Published 2025

Cover Art by Ellen "Elf" Sack

LIBRARY OF CONGRESS CATALOGING-IN-PUBLICATION DATA

Foreman, Stephen / Home: A Love Story / First Edition

Fiction, General. Fiction, Autofiction.

ISBN: 979-8-9924613-2-9 (Trade Paperback)

Printed in the United States of America

For Dorian

HOME:

A Love Story

Stephen H. Foreman

ALTERNATIVE BOOK PRESS

Contents

Chapter 1

Poppa: Gain in Loss

I was raised in Poppa's house, barely born when grandpa became Poppa and Grandma Sophie Rose was still alive. My mother was their daughter. My father was career Marine Corps—Intelligence, MOS 0231—a captain stationed in the Middle East. Mom called him Dear Skipper. When she was pregnant with me, she flew over to give birth in the base hospital. I guess the medical facilities were excellent there.

I was one month old when they strapped me into my car seat for a little spin. Their car hit a tank mine near the border. Killed them both. I didn't have a scratch. Poppa flew over and brought us all home. He said when he first took me in his arms that I was both a joy and a sorrow. He said he knew that joy would grow but his sorrow would stay put. He said my name suited me—Thea—Gift of God. Imagine. Not a scratch. Thea.

Poppa didn't talk much about my grandmother, or my mom. Once, when I asked about my mom, he said, "You want to know about your mother? Look in the mirror. You're her. Your mother was like her mother, and you are like yours."

"That's it?"

"That's it."

"That's not it."

"That's it for now."

Poppa stopped right there in his tracks, like he nosed up against a French door. Some strange noise emanated from deep in his throat, deeper down, I believe, than guts ought to go.

"What, Poppa?", I asked, truly concerned. He'd lost color, too.

"If Botticelli had painted Venus with black hair and green eyes...the Irish in her. Madden, McFadden, Flaherty, Donnelly. Her family names. Could be a long-haul trucker law firm, couldn't it? Sophie Rose McFadden. You can hear the rhythm of those Irish drums in those names. She arrived from a world that wasn't ours."

"You were lucky."

"Was I?"

"You had her."

"We win. We lose."

"It's one helluva price."

"What?"

"Love."

"What's the price?"

"Grief."

"Ecstasy."

"Here's to it."

"Small price to pay," he said.

My life changed his. He might as well have been shut off. His job was me and that was that. Whatever else he was doing, which was a lot, he stopped—the lectures, consulting jobs, projects in foreign places, occasional articles for trade journals, state dinners, hobnobbing— "I didn't give up anything," he'd say. "I traded up." He'd eaten in some of the finest restaurants in the world and a few of the worst. Try finding a good deli in Chad.

"Been there. Done that. Now I'm doing this," was his way. "I'd rather have a tuna salad on sourdough toast, fries, and a vanilla coke at the Come-On-Inn." Our local diner. "Nouveau cuisine? The least amount of food for the most amount of money? Fourteen bucks for a braised carrot? Pass."

"Don't look back," he quoted the great Satchel Paige, "It might be gainin' on ya." Poppa never looked back. I didn't know enough to miss my mom and dad, but Poppa's been there. I remember a little girl from elementary school who said, "Your father's got white hair. When's he gonna die?"

"Never," I said, warning her she'd best stand back three feet or more.

Of course, I don't remember a thing but, by the time Poppa brought me home from Kuwait, Aunt Gert had finished decorating my baby room. I have pictures of it: lush, green walls covered with flowers and bumblebees, butterflies, and a weeping cherry tree. Spider plants hung from the windows. Little Miss Muffet Sat on A Tuffet. Fruit burst from a succulent. I was raised in a garden. Fine with me.

Fall and Poppa were both born by the same breath. Fall was our favorite season. We braved the freeze of winter, the muck of spring, and the sweat of summer, until we got to Fall. It was Fall when Poppa was most alive, and, because he was, I was, too. Poppa may have been biologically my grandpops, my grandfather, but he was the only father I've ever known. I called him Poppa early on and have done so ever since. When I was little, I rode Poppa's back through a blueberry jungle in August. It seemed I was always riding Poppa's back somewhere, across a stream bed, around a snowdrift, the world from Poppa's back. Somebody once said about him, "Underneath that harsh exterior beats a heart of Cream of Wheat." That's my Poppa right on.

I never have been a big fan of Summer. Born and raised in a cleft in the Catskill Mountains when they were still home and hearth to dogged farmers tilling fields whose main crop was rocks. This was way before the hipsters from Brooklyn donned their L.L. Bean backpacks crammed with gorp and holy water, and discovered we lived here. I don't dispute that summer in the mountains is lovely – fulsome creeks fished by blue herons and eagles, thickets shielding deer, partridge, and bear, goldenrod and purple astor, so many shades of green, but, still, for me, mercifully short. It's a season that can't be avoided and creates an obligation to hungrily suck it dry of all its pleasures right down to the last hot dog on the grill and that August mountain thunderstorm right above your head. I do, but I won't lie—that first chill wind and the changing colors soon after—that's what I wait for. Maple syrup, pumpkins, and the palette a hardwood forest offers in the Fall—maple, ash, beech, oak, black cherry, walnut, chestnut— an opera of joyful shades—basso basso profundo coloratura - bronze, orange, red, yellow. I know from firsthand experience that Alaskan hardwoods are small and stunted. There are no beauty queens on the tundra. It's so cold that leaves and roots become necessities. Wood, the stuff of trunks and branches, is a luxury. I look at the mountains across my valley and it's like looking at a bouquet. "Here y'go, Thea. This one's for you."

Growing up, every year, and even now sometimes when I'm back, me and Poppa kick through the cover of dry leaves on the ground whenever we walk through the woods along Hunter Creek in the Fall. I remember one October morning, a young spruce, maybe three feet, sparsely but gracefully branched, decorated by wind and gravity, holding brightly colored leaves that had fallen from other trees. It was not the burning bush, but it dazzled. Our mountains are part of the range that goes south into West Virginia and Kentucky, all the Appalachians. Oh, my, the aroma of fresh, rich mud – better than morning coffee – that came from those walks. Life was in those kicks. Even the sound – that crispness – that snap, crackle, and pop of leaves so casually scuffed aside! To walk through those woods in the Fall was to experience transcendence. I'm not talking religion here, but I know that feeling when I feel it. It envelops me and whispers to me, though I never quite catch the words. Like something I can almost remember, a sad thing and a happy thing, not birthday party happy—more of an astonished kind of happy—and not a terrible kind of sad but more of a longing. Feels like peace but also a piece of the puzzle: tranquil and untroubled, and yet something I urgently needed to know but it's just out of reach. How could it be that with every breath I was both aroused and at rest? How could that be? I remember leaving the woods of that childhood at dusk, and above me the moon was full and bright, serene, imposing: Buddha. How could that be?

It was Fall, first day of school, but we had plans.

Poppa knocked on my door when it was still more than an hour from daybreak.

"Bacon, sunny sides, hash browns, hot chocolate. Hit the deck." Poppa hawked from the other side of the door. "Dress warm."

I had my warmest clothes all laid out, layers of 'em. I felt like the Michelin tire man, but it was gonna be cold out there. In the Spring you smell fresh flowers, but in the Fall, you smell dead ones, crisp and sour. The season has a tang to it.

Poppa showed me a wild apple tree. A Macoun. His secret. Nobody else knew where it was, and how it got where it got even Poppa couldn't say.

"They talk to each other, y'know, not like we do, but think of all those tangled roots mingling underground, connecting like telephone cables. Information gets passed on through. All these oaks? They weren't here when you were born. Logged out. But all this time they've been migrating down the mountain and look at them now. Maybe they send out pilgrims to scout new territory? Like anybody would. 'Course, I'm no botanist, so wha' do I know?" Poppa said that after a lot of things, "Wha' do I know?" But he knew just about everything, and, if there was a speck of something he didn't know, he'd find somebody who did or look it up or just go and figure it out for himself. He'd pick up a bronze leaf and tell me oak, a red leaf, maple, a yellow leaf, birch, a different red, sumac. Wild berries had been gone for a month, but pears and apples were in, and a pumpkin patch he planted just for me, tiny pumpkins, and really big ones, hundred pounders, a patch the size of a swimming pool. That patch made my Halloweens even more magical. Every Halloween we'd choose the second biggest and carve a monster mug, scary being the operative word. The first biggest, the biggest of all, we saved for when I was Cinderella and needed my coach.

With a bellyful of breakfast, Aunt Gert stuffed egg salad sandwiches into the pockets of our red and black wool hunting jackets.

"Aren't you supposed to be in school?" she asked.

"She is in school," said Poppa.

"I am in school," I said.

"I didn't ask you," said Aunt Gertie

"Yes, you did," I said.

Aunt Gert shut the door behind us, called the dogs to join her, and dove back under her quilts.

We set off over the back field towards the tree line, a special spot Poppa had picked out a few weeks earlier. all by the light of a slender sickle moon. He had his ancient shotgun with him, a turn of the century, Remington Model 1889 10-gauge double barrel. Worth a fortune, he'd told me; it had been his father's and his father's. He could've afforded a new one, but never bought one. Poppa said it could damn near shoot itself. Poppa was once quoted in an interview saying, "If you don't own a gun and you don't own a book, what good are you?" He actually said that. It was the caption under a picture of him grinning like he'd won $5,000 a month from Publisher's Clearing House. I think he was joking.

No matter how hard I tried not to make any noise, withered grass sheathed in ice crackled underfoot. Poppa had taught me how the Mohawks walked while hunting, slowly, setting the whole foot down gently, one single gradual movement instead of heel-toe-heel. My feet still went crunch crunch, as I walked. Poppa wore moccasins and made no sound at all.

Up in the blackest sky I'd yet ever seen, the moon had shrunk to a slice. The stars were tingles of light cluttering the sky. I got thinking about the wandering bands of early humans. How much of their lives were spent staring up at the stars? It was the best quiz show in their universe. Stories flowed. Ideas flourished. Mathematics was born. Directions were set.

I don't know how he did it, but, when we crossed the tree line into the woods, it was so black I thought I went blind, only Poppa didn't seem bothered one bit. Off over to the side somewhere, the hogs were already on the move nuzzling for chinkapins. Might be some wild ones with 'em. Poppa beckoned me keep quiet. We didn't want to set them off and spoil the whole thing. Pass on by. Shhh. Poppa veered off a bit. I could just make out an old maple tree, thick like a pillar on an ancient temple. You couldn't miss it, trunk warped and twisted all the way up with large boles like warts. Something so sweet once came from that tree. Poppa pointed to the ground. I sat down, my back against that scratchy bark. Poppa cut brush and fashioned a blind, then sat down next to me. He put his finger to his lips, took three long, slim bones from a leather pouch hanging from his belt. Call bones. Thin, graceful, harp-like. Call bones he'd had since he was a kid. Cup them to your lips and talk turkey.

With the shotgun in the crook of his arm, Poppa arranged the bones in the palm of his hand, cupped them to his mouth, and what came out was a *puk puk puk,* a sweet chirp almost impossible to hear. *Puk puk puk.* I listened hard but all I could hear was quiet. I think Poppa mighta winked at me. Not sure. The next one just fluttered out, some sweet *puk puks*, lilting *chirps*, and *tra la trills*. A symphony of bones. I listened hard. The silence was thick and firm. Then, oh my God, I heard this *boom boom boom* coming towards us. *Boom boom boom!* Heavy wings beating on the ground. Might've been Godzilla. Poppa gave a final, *puk puk trill cluk*, and the most humongous turkey on earth busted through the brush smack into the clearing in front of our blind. Stout as a sergeant major. He came to a stop, stood at attention, and looked around. Poppa gave it one more lick. That big dandy fanned out his bodacious tail—a thing of beauty if you ever see one—an emperor -- danced and pranced in a circle and made right for us.

The shotgun jumped to Poppa's shoulder and fired. That bird went down like a running back clotheslined by a safety. Whop. Down. Poppa didn't move. One wing fluttered then fell still. Might've been the wind. We waited for the echo of the shot to fade away and then sat still some more. It goes so quiet in the woods when a hunter—man or beast—takes prey. Something about that silence says you must sit still for a while. I got up when Poppa got up, and we walked to where the bird had fallen. Poppa knelt to check the bird's spurs, big ones, long, sharp, a good two inches. He didn't say one word for a bit until, with as much reverence as I'd ever heard him, he stood, bowed his head, and said: *"Been a bad old booger, but he's come and gone."*

Chapter 2

Aunt Gert— Driving Home –Present Day

Driving is a good time for dreaming. Tires churn things up. I was headed home for some serious R & R in the mountains. My plane was hours late getting into Boston, stupid stuff, like we had to disembark because they forgot to weigh the plane without passengers. Does anybody out there even know they do that? Anyway, I was bone tired and just wanted to go to sleep in my own bed. Nurses Without Borders had sent me up to the Yukon giving measles vaccinations and flu shots to kids in isolated Athapaskan villages, Eagle and Circle being two of them. Sometimes I need to get as far away as I can get, but it's good to have something productive to do once I'm there.

"Home is where when you have to go there, they have to take you in." Robert Frost. I don't mean to be pretentious, but I was a lit minor in college. More to the point, such a cynical point of view, true, I guess, for lots of people, but not for me. I was always welcome, and, even though I yearned to get away, I yearned just as badly to get back.

When we finally landed after an unexpected and unexplained stop somewhere in the boonies of Saskatchewan, I was too worn out to drive the two hundred plus miles to the northern Catskills. Home. I picked up my car and spent the night at a friend's place near Boston, Lexington, actually, where I detoxed with one too many of the shots heard 'round the world.

Aunt Gert first called me when I was in the shower, so I didn't hear the ring. Next time she called, I was struggling to grab a towel and get to my phone, dropped the phone while trying to hit talk.

"Hey, Thea, that you? You there? Thea. Thea! Pick the hell up."

"I'm here. I'm here."

"Why aren't you *here*?"

"Because I didn't want to die on the highway last night."

"It's Aunt Gert."

"No kidding."

Aunt Gert, Poppa's baby sister, moved up from West Virginia to help out Poppa and my grandmother when my mother was born. Most of the rest of the Jews had long ago vacated those parts. When Sophie Rose, my grandmother, was killed, Aunt Gert stayed on to help raise me to the mensch I am today. She's been my mother most of my life. The house stayed a mess, and the food she cooked was mostly just alright, but she loved me so deeply and so happily that what else mattered? A little dust? Well, a lot of dust. So, what?

Aunt Gert's hillbilly ways were just as suited to rural New York. She could've specialized in snake handling, referred to herself as a "Heeb Billy", and could make the best apple pie blintzes on earth. She'd butcher your deer for you, too. She could even do it kosher if you wanted—kept a separate set of knives, Japanese steel, not a nick—and play her some Tammy Wynette while doing it. If a person could be short and lanky all at once, she was, with a red face like she picked cotton all day under a hot sun.

"On my way. Just got out of the shower," I said.

"They got showers in igloos?"

"You sound like a damn redneck."

"I am a damn redneck."

"You are the sister and aunt of Jewish intelligentsia."

"Intelligentsi-i. You won't believe this one."

"Try me."

"State Police—Trooper Colby? —You know him—he's been here before. We get a call, come get Poppa. They had him at the station. He'd gone down to the highway, stretched a logging chain across the road. Sat down behind it on a barrel with a shotgun across his lap, said he had that old dog of his right there by his side, old Buster Fleabag—remember him? — but it was just a clip of Buster's hair Poppa always carries in that little leather pouch. Wasn't no dog there. You know that. Trooper Colby was really nice to Poppa."

"Whatcha doin', Poppa?", Colby asked kindly.

"Keepin' the furriners out," Poppa said, deadly serious.

"I believe the country's grateful for your service, Sir, but it's safe to go now. We got everything under control."

Poppa asked him if he was sure and Colby assured him, he was, then Poppa thanked him and just went along, no problem. They called me to come down to the station house to fetch him. I got there, he and Colby were playing chess."

"Where's Poppa now?"

"Back home. Workin' on another bird house."

"What's it this time?"

"The Taj."

"Majal?"

"You know another Taj?"

Poppa was Michelangelo with wood. At some point, he decided he wanted to create bird houses in the form of classical structures, like the Taj, but also St. Peter's in Rome, Stonehenge outside of London, Ellis Island in New York harbor, the Bastille in Paris, France, and such, even a termite mound and an Apache wickiup. Sold them for a fortune. If something struck him, he'd find a way to do it. If something didn't, he wouldn't. You never could figure out what Poppa was going to do next, even, they tell me, when he was younger, but what he would do mostly made some sense if you thought about it much, which I did.

Poppa had been all over the world, seen so much, took it all in. He didn't just see what he saw, he thought hard about it: who built it; why; materials used; materials quarried. He saw what was never written, the souls of the folks who thought of these things, the souls of the people who needed these things, the lives of the workers who laid the stones at the tops of tall towers, the thousand-year myths that gave rise to it all. He never just visited places, he worked in them—dug wells, taught school, tilled fields, held babies, dug bodies out of mudslides, repaired roofs shredded by monsoons.

Poppa was a civil engineer by training, a doer of good deeds by constitution. He dreamed of building roads where there weren't any. Poppa constructed bridges where there were only ropes stretched across immense gorges that would swallow you with a single slip. He discovered an entire network of roads leading to an abandoned village site deep in the jungle of Honduras. And the man was not shy. He loved to talk about the stuff he did and got himself registered on the speaker's circuit. If Jane Goodall could do it, so good he.

But he was smart in another way, too, that *yiddishe kopf* of his. He thought carefully and invested well, like IBM at twenty-two dollars per share. McDonald's was twenty-two bucks a share as well. He saw the future, at

16

least, a piece of it. It made it easier for him to do what he wanted the way he wanted to do it without taking crap from anybody.

*

"Hey, Thea, where'd you go?" yelled Aunt Gert.

"Here," I answered.

"Grab me a six pack when you stop for gas. Budweiser. Not that seditty stuff you drink."

"Bud light?"

"You do and you're outta the will."

"You've got a will?"

"I'll get one."

"'On the road again,'" I sang.

"Let's surprise the old man."

"Done deal."

*

Out of all Poppa's siblings, Aunt Gert was the liveliest. She danced. She sang. She knew the songs. She knew the steps. First to be invited to parties.

First to set a style. And then she broke out with acne, terrible pustules oozing green. Painful. Humiliating. Aunt Gert wouldn't leave the house. Her parents finally took her to a specialist who recommended x-ray treatments. It was experimental, but Aunt Gert insisted they "get this filth off my face." Treatment commenced and her acne disappeared, but the x-rays burned her right cheek leaving her with a brown patch like a wrinkled waffle. She never went to another party, rarely left the house unless she had to, stopped singing and dancing, jettisoned the joy.

Aunts don't get much better than Aunt Gert. She lived with us but, still, every time she saw me it was like the first time ever, giving me a huge smile and a sloppy kiss. Poppa used to joke, "Gert with the short skirt." I think he said it nearly every time she walked into the room. She would tell me things about my mom and dad and Poppa and Grandma that Poppa never did talk about.

"That shindig in Washington Square Park? The Summer of Love? Your Poppa met your grandmother and got arrested the same night. He'd been recently discharged from the Marine Corps and was in New York City looking for work. His haircut was still regulation - high and tight - and he sported a new blue suit he'd purchased at Robert Hall, oxford blue button-down shirt, rep tie, wing tips, argyle socks. He thought he'd done well in his interviews, so he took himself down to Little Italy to celebrate at Umberto's Clam House hoping to get a glimpse of Joey Gallo, the notorious mobster, who'd bragged, "I got one foot in the grave, and the other on a roller skate." This would prove true years later when he was assassinated with his mouth open and his next portion of pasta vongole already on his fork. When the guy was finally gunned down, Poppa wondered if they'd both sat at the same table. Your Poppa had always wanted to eat there, so he treated himself, a huge portion of pasta with clams, and the house wine, of course. Dessert? Cannoli.

Afterward, he decided to walk back to his hotel room. He had to go through Washington Square Park which was packed with anti-war demonstrators— skinny girls with hairy pits, white guys with dreadlocks, pig signs, guitars— as he pushed his way through the mob, he became angrier and angrier. Aunt Gert said Poppa believed the war was wrong. But "Once a Marine, always a Marine." That gut truth would never go away for him. He'd trained hard, learned the ways of war, and faced difficulties those people had never dreamed of. He found himself hating the sight of them, the smell of them, their voices, and knew he would blow if he didn't get away from there. He needed to settle down behind a beer and a burger. Your Poppa knew his fuse was short and did not want to explode, so he found this place, one of those spots where you order at a counter and they call your name when your food is ready. He ordered, found a table, sat down and waited. The place was filled with men and women, all of them straight from the peace demonstration. The counterman calls Poppa's name so Poppa goes to get his order and takes it back to his seat. He passed a girl who could have been a model from the Renaissance sitting at a table by her lonesome. They look at each other, smile, and say hello."

"You were at the demonstration," she said.

"Sort of."

"Sort of what?"

"I wasn't dressed for it."

"Funny."

"Meant to be. I'm Reuben Henry."

"I'm Sophie Rose McFadden. Glad to meet you, Reuben Henry."

Aunt Gert said Poppa told her all this after she sent bail money by Western Union.

"So, this guy comes up to him, probably Sophie Rose's date, tricked out like a Harley rider with a peace sign on the back of his jacket and long blonde dreads. "Can I help you?" asks this guy."

"No. I'm fine, thank you."

"What's with the suit and haircut?"

"Bad fit?"

"Where'd you get it?"

"Robert Hall. Like it?"

"The haircut."

"Courthouse Bay."

"Where's that?"

"North Carolina."

"Where?"

"Camp Lejeune."

The way Poppa told it this guy had some kind of freak implosion, like Poppa was some kind of suppurating leper.

"What're you doing here?" asks the guy.

"Having a burger and fries. Nice to meet you, Sophie Rose." Poppa turns away to go to his table.

"Is that where you learned to kill babies?"

So, Poppa stops and turns around and says, "Don't."

"How many babies did you kill?"

"You don't want to do this."

"So, this guy gets right up in Poppa's face—all smug and sarcastic—says, 'Napalm? Rocket fire? Fixed bayonets?'" "So, Poppa turns his back on this guy and begins to walk to his table."

"You're a big man with your M-16 and your baby killing buddies all around you,' the guy says. People had started watching them. So, Poppa turns around again and says, 'You've been listening to too many Waylon Jennings' records, asshole.' So, this guy goes ballistic because he's been called an asshole with his lady listening, so, of course, peace 'n' love notwithstanding, he's gotta do something."

"How are you one on one?" the man taunts, and morphs into some whacko Bruce Lee pose replete with sound effects. Yi! Yi! You know the one. Well, Miss Thea, you don't press your Poppa. Poppa cracked the guy in the kidney, and the jerk-wad went down."

"Nice to meet you," Poppa says to the young lady still sitting at the table.

"Nice to meet you, too," she said back.

"But before your Poppa could say another word, he was jumped by three bouncers who restrained him until the cops arrived, put him in cuffs, and took him away. It didn't help that the guy on the floor was spitting blood. Poppa was charged with aggravated assault and battery, but once the cards were shuffled and the truth came out, the charges were dropped."

"Who was that woman? Sophie Rose. Sophie Rose who? Sophie Rose McWhat? McFadden. Aunt Gert said it was Poppa's Big Bang! The entirety of his DNA imploded in under a nanosecond: Poppa desired to spend every minute of the rest of his entire life with this creature who'd completely snatched his heart. There it was. How does something so unreasonable seem so sane, so right, so cosmically correct? Poppa was in love, only he didn't know who he was in love with or where to find her. What he did was begin to hang out where they first met. He sat there for days on end, hamburger after hamburger, onion rings and fries, until the evening she walked in. With the same guy! They walked to a table. Before they sat down Reuben Henry approached them. The guy went white. Poppa raised his hands in gentle surrender and said, "Peace 'n' love, brother." then held out his arm for Sophie Rose 'til death did them part."

"They had their tussles, like everybody, but the deep connect was always there. When her eyes closed for the evening, so did his. When he reached for her hand while they slept, she reached for his. They dreamt together. Main thing was she did not want him to do anything unreasonably dangerous, which he did or dreamed of doing all the time, unless of course, she did it with him. Her caveat. He liked to go places other people didn't. Ask him why, he'd shrug and say," Just curious." They finally settled on their MO. "I'm like Ruth from the Bible, whither thou goest, know what I mean, jellybean?" If he were going to be wherever, then she was going to be wherever, too. With him. Together. Or somewhere close. Like the best hotel. Period. End of sentence. He wanted to be able to look at her face every morning whether in Borneo or Battle Creek, Michigan. They did this for years before your mother was born. Once she was here, they didn't want to go anywhere else. Of course, Poppa did from time to time, but rarely, your grandma almost never. Their home had been in her family for over a hundred years, the stone foundation a century before that. Sophie Rose's one demand were they to marry: "I want to raise our daughter where I was raised.'"

"When your mother was born, Sophie Rose was quite happy to be home, and quite busy with that home, only going elsewhere if it were important, which most things were not. Then something came along she couldn't resist, and it killed her. That was not the first time your grandfather had to fly remains home from another country. When your mother was killed, he had you to think about. No time to wallow. You were tiny. Five pounds if that? You needed him, and he needed you. He stood back and watched you grow. Never turned away. You got so much of him in you."

Chapter 3

Floyd & Lloyd & Sophie Rose

Sophie Rose's profession was a blend of art and archaeology. She'd become an expert on cave paintings and had studied all the important sites - Canyon de Chelly, the Canyonlands - that one that went on for nine miles - Lascaux - all of them. Thea's grandmother had developed a theory that posited artificial light used by archaeologists when exploring caves did not illuminate the paintings like the light of ancient torches. Such flickering light made the animals appear as moving, running, jumping, not standing still with hunters pursuing them.

"After a lifetime of happily galloping around the world, once your mother was born, your grandmother never wanted to leave," Poppa told Thea. "Normally, Floyd and Lloyd, twin brothers in their nineties, locals born and bred, watched over your grandmother whenever I had to go off on a necessary junket. So, when a new cave was discovered in northern Yemen, a cave unlike any found in that part of the world before, your grandmother was offered a foundation grant to study it with an international team. These ancient artists climbed towards a ledge eighteen feet above the cave floor. The paintings began there. She couldn't turn down that kind of opportunity—I told her, *Go with God.   I'd keep the home fires burning. Floyd. Lloyd. Gert with the short skirt. Don't worry about us.* And off she went."

"We held hands while waiting for the car that was sent to take her to the airport. We kissed. She got into the car, and we waved to each other as the car pulled away. That was it. I never saw her again," Poppa said, his voice breaking. "She hadn't been gone very long when the sun came up one morning and nobody could find her. When she still hadn't shown up by the next day, a search was organized. It went on for weeks until her remains were found, mostly eaten away by wild creatures, not much left, but still enough to   determine she'd been strangled to death. Who'd done it? Why? To have survived a lifetime and then die like that.

"So, you raised my mother, and now you're raising me," I said.

"Karma," Poppa replied, "Actually, more you than her. I still had to earn a living back then."

"You won the lottery," I joked.

"Like I said, Toots, karma. I'm being punished for some unspeakable sin I committed in another life."

"You are not."

"Okay, I'm not," Poppa said with a grin and a wink. "One time, I don't know where it came from or why, I saved your grandmother's life. You wouldn't be here. I'd have missed it all. She could've died right there in front of me. If I'd lost her, I would've wanted to die myself. We kinda had our honeymoon first because the day after the wedding we were going to be in different parts of the world. I was at a conference on St. Lucia—the illegal trafficking of exotic species. She was in Acoma observing their ancient process of firing pottery. The plan was to meet up on St. Lucia then island hop to St. Vincent and spend a week on a volcanic black sand beach. At that time, nobody wanted to lie around on black sand, so the place was pretty much isolated, perfect for the two of us. From the top of the cliff, we could hear waves thundering into the caverns below, exploding against the rocks. Nobody there but us."

"One problem. Your grandmother had gotten sick but travelled, anyway. Doc told her not to, but your grandma had her own MO. Her plan, unknown to me, of course, was to ask me to marry her while she was there—when I least expected it. I'd been asking her daily for years. It had become a joke. Neither of us was going anywhere, and we both knew it. Anyway, my Sophie Rose had this plan. You're talking one determined lady. She was resolute. Do it. Did it."

"When I first saw her back at the hotel, she looked like the sickest version of herself I could imagine. It was frightening. Skin like chalk. I knew people on St. Vincent who were the descendants of the original British settlers. Phyllis Punnett had even written the St. Vincentian national anthem. They got her to a doctor as soon as we landed. Kiddo, she was so sick—just awful—scared the crap out of me. The doctor diagnosed *quincy*. Who the hell knew what that was, but her throat had closed up, and if it didn't begin to open up in twenty-four hours, the doctor would need to open her airway with pvc pipe. PVC Pipe! Down her throat. Not what one would call a cutting-edge medical technique. That's all your grandma needed to hear. Twenty-four hours later, the swelling had gone down, still there, but on the way out."

"What she had—get this—was an *otolaryngologic emergency. Acute epiglottitis.* That flap in your throat that keeps food from going into the lungs? Swollen like a billiard ball. She'd clapped her hands over her ears, but I listened carefully as the doctor described it as an accumulation of pus, due to an infection behind the tonsils, PTA, peritonsillar abscess. Aren't you happy to know this? George Washington died of quincy. Took him twenty-one hours."

"We went to the beach as soon as she felt better. She said she didn't want to waste another day. What we didn't know was the water where we were headed was known for being unpredictable and dangerous, but we got there and in she went. Your grandmother was a strong swimmer. I was right behind her. Water has never been my go-to medium. I can swim if I need to, but I'd rather not. I was a little queasy because she'd gone out further than I would've liked. We were separated by maybe ten feet when I realized she was in trouble. She was trying to swim back in but couldn't, didn't have the strength to fight her way forward through the backwash. And then she began slipping backwards. I could see her fighting to go forward but she couldn't. She was going to drown. I yelled to her but she didn't hear me. I launched myself toward her, managed to reach her, and timed a huge wave as it was coming in, pushed her up by her butt onto the crest of that wave which catapulted her forward to where she could swim to safety."

"That left me. When I struck out for the beach and could not do it, could not fight free no matter how hard I tried. Useless. I did not want to die. In the instant, I decided if my next stroke didn't take me forward, I was going to lie on my back, stay calm, and allow the current to carry me to a safe place (which eventually it would have, provided I didn't drown or get eaten. Well, I lunged hard and did break free. My Sophie Rose was waiting for me on the beach."

"Yo ho ho and a bottle of rum," your grandmother sang. "Let's celebrate!"

"You could've died two times in one day," I told her.

 Her reply? "Y'think that's a record?"

"My god. I just loved that woman," Poppa said to me. "An original. And she chose me! This singular selection of molecules chose me! She had her choice, and she chose me. *What A Wonderful World* - thank you, Satchmo."

Chapter 4

The Breakfast Nook

I only know that summer sang in me a little while that sings in me no more.

When I was growing up, we had a breakfast nook in a recess in one corner of our kitchen. A small rectangle of a table, light blue with red trim, and two benches with backs on either side. Aunt Gert painted bright, yellow sunflowers on it. Poppa and I had most of our serious talks there, usually late at night. Our "midnight snack". We'd eat slugs off a Hebrew National salami and wash them down with ginger ale. One such night, he said I could ask him anything as long as he could reserve the right not to answer.

"Then I don't have to answer either," I declared.

"Wrong," he said, "You gotta be twenty-one in this state to legally answer a question. You got a good dozen years to go. If I let you get away without an answer, the cops could put me in the slammer."

I figured that one out way before twenty-one.

"When you were born," Poppa told me, "You had me mesmerized from the git-go. What if I hadn't walked through Washington Square that day, met such an exceptional lady, and punched out her boyfriend? And, as if it wasn't enough, finding my Sophie Rose, your mother came along and I swore she was the most beautiful creature in all creation. Then you, my dear, were born—whammo! —right up there with the angels. When I saw your face—I was looking at your mother's face. I was looking at your grandmother's face. Your ol' Poppa was a goner, three times, in no time. One look. One tiny, mini, nano-sec. I didn't need more."

Home. I drove, smiling at the memory. Another memory surfaced, I wasn't even four, before I could read or write, me sneaking down to that nook at night, using my finger to draw in the air above the nook. Designs, squiggles, colors, words (not really, but what she thought were words). They were invisible, of course, but I was absolutely convinced that all these drawings would appear in the air over the nook on Christmas morning, which was weird considering we're Jewish and don't celebrate Christmas. But   Lloyd and Floyd did, and I loved visiting their house at Christmastime, napping under their tree.

I woke up while it was still dark, expecting to see a carnival of colors floating in the air above the nook on Christmas morning. I didn't want to wake anyone, so I used my flashlight to run downstairs to the nook. At first, half-asleep, I thought I saw squiggles, circles, and dots. Colors I'd invented. Words I'd made up. Yay! Hooray! Yippee! And then I blinked.

Um…

What happened to them?

There was nothing up there but air, empty air, not one squiggle, no colors at all, not even a dot. I longed to see my masterpiece, and when I told Poppa, he said I must've made it with disappearing ink. That's what Poppa told me. He had a friend in the CIA who told him all about it. "No wonder..." he laughed. "You used disappearing ink. A very magical kind. Only goblins with special glasses can see it." When I was young, with Poppa, it seemed he always knew what to do. When I was young and with Poppa, I was safe.

The evening before I left for boot camp, we sat at the breakfast nook and talked. Poppa got real serious.

"I loved you, Thea, before I set eyes on you. I loved your grandmother before I ever met her. Did I somehow know you both already? You were words and feelings and wishes, poems and paintings, dandelions on the lawn, Jupiter, Venus, and full moons—all kinds of adventures conjured up and stored away—white water, temple bells. I knew I would show her the calm of the desert, the chatter of a mountain creek, words that mattered…all the things I loved. And she showed me all that she loved, and we loved it all together. I knew you and I would cuddle on the sofa watching *Bambi*. I knew one day we'd have these midnight snacks of ours. Before you were here, who were you, and who was she? I could feel love gesturing although I didn't yet know what would become of what I was feeling. It's as if I set up a bank account of love to save for the day when my need for those deposits would become the monthly payments on my life."

"That's heavy," I said. "You're a poet Poppa."

Poppa looked amused. "I loved your mother dearly. She became a feminist at the age of three. Hands on hips. *"You're not the boss of me."* Laying down the law. Right on, young lady. I couldn't have loved her more. She was my daughter, our daughter, the shared blood of the love of my life. Even so, there was still a place in me that was empty." Poppa didn't say anything for a good long while, didn't move. I don't know where he went but he wasn't here with me. I wanted to reach out and touch him but knew I should wait. Finally, he said,

"I'd rather be your grandfather than *ganze macher* of a gazillion dollar private equity outfit. Private. Shmivate. Outfit. Shmoutfit. It was a very dirty job but somebody had to do it. We asked for a show of hands. There weren't any."

"Funny."

"Apparently, I missed my calling."

"Regrets?"

"Regrets? I never had my own stand-up gig in Vegas. On the other hand, I must've been an attorney general in another life. I'd put that goddamn private equity den of thieves behind bars. Forget those poor schmucks smashing windows. You want looters? Forget baseball bats. Take up your Mont Blanc pens. Parasites. Eats its host from the inside out. And you're worried about a TV set? Don't get me started."

"You're already started."

"My father used to say I'd have a rude awakening. The sixties gave us hope, but I think he felt there was none. For him, that was true. He was crippled with a disease that would kill him."

"People say your generation was naive."

"You had to be naive to pull those stunts. A bunch of Hippies sit in the balcony of the Stock Exchange - our Free Market Valhalla - and toss real dollar bills onto the trading floor. Scrunch 'em up and toss 'em or fold 'em into paper airplanes and launch 'em. Cut 'em into bits. Tossed like confetti. Throwing money away while the mites below were scrambling to make it. I'd say that's number one on today's list of naive political stunts. Wait a minute. How 'bout this one? Levitating the Pentagon! Thousands and thousands surrounding the building and chanting and chanting and chanting. Ommmmmmm. Ommmmmm. Ommmmmmm. The largest tie dye gathering in history! They believed they could make it rise from the ground!"

"But it didn't."

"The technique hadn't been perfected, yet."

"It *hasn't* been perfected, yet."

"That, too.

Chapter 5

Aunt Gert Steps Out

One time a man kept coming to the door for her. Aunt Gert tried shooing him away but finally let him in. They bumped into each other at the supermarket, although he later admitted he did it on purpose so he could meet her. His name was Sid. Sid had been places. Told a good joke, too. Brought Aunt Gert flowers and fancy candy. Softened her heart, although a Baby Ruth was just fine with her. Took her to three different restaurants - Mexican, Chinese, and Italian - when she hadn't even been to the local diner in years. He let her drive his car, a tricked out DeSoto, the size of a gunboat. She let him take her to a drive-in movie.

I really liked Sid. He could do card tricks, got me chocolate covered pretzels, and told me I was growing up a really good kid.

"You like him?" asked Poppa.

"He'll do," Aunt Gertie answered.

"I asked if you *like* him."

"No, I don't like him, damn it, but he'll do!"

"Do for what?"

"Two from column A. One from column B."

"Make mine dumplings."

*

One day, Sid had a bad headache, a migraine. Seeing triple. Aunt Gert said he was sure popping a lot of those Percodans. She'd checked his medicine chest.

"Gertrude, would you please deliver this package for me?"

She told me she loved the way he said her name. The package was for a buyer, he told her. *Money's already in the bank. Just drop it off and come right back.* She'd have to drive to Albany, but it was doable, and so she did it. A very nice man took the package from her at the door. He offered her coffee before she drove back, but she was anxious to get home.

Sid had already left, but she'd see him in the morning. In the morning, instead of Sid, she saw the police. They had our house surrounded. Aunt Gert, thinking she was delivering pottery samples from a village in Honduras, delivered two kilos of the purest cocaine to an address known to the authorities. She was photographed. Her car was photographed. Her license plate was photographed. Sid had disappeared. Aunt Gert was cuffed and jailed. Poppa bailed her out. Everyone in the valley vouched for her. She was suckered. A con man preyed on her. No charges were brought.

Sid's DeSoto turned out to be stolen from another state and was found abandoned in an auto graveyard. Aunt Gert's heart wasn't broken, but the primitive portion of her brain itched for a violent and bloody revenge. Poppa warned she was gonna eat herself up, but we could see it was hard to shake. God help that man if she saw him in that stupid supermarket again. She increased her trips to the market, bought what she didn't need. She didn't even like sardines, but every time she went to that market, she prayed that he'd come in for a quart of milk, a pound of butter, chocolate chip cookies...anything, anything at all. Just get your slimy ass in here, and I'll take care of all the rest. Of course, he never did, so she never did.

"Thea," she said to me, "There are two kinds of men in this world: bastards and skunks." In her dreams, she shredded them without mercy, but awake she made herself so sick she had to go to the hospital and stay there for a while. I was packing some of her things to take to her when I found the underwear that Poppa kept complaining were always getting lost. "How the hell do Jockey shorts get lost? They walk away by themselves?" Well, case solved. The Jockey shorts never did get lost. Aunt Gert had been wearing them. I couldn't find any underwear of her own. She never bought any. Why would she? Poppa's fit.

The house was so quiet without her. Aunt Gert was a proponent for the greatest good. She could be a pain in the ass, but she mostly was up for the party, figuratively speaking. We laughed a lot. She thought I was funny, and I thought she was funny. Sometimes she made my ribs hurt. She taught me important things such as when you have to go to a public bathroom, like in the department store, flush the handle with your foot. She waged a lifelong war against her only sworn enemy, except for the weasel who conned her, germs. Aunt Gert went through a brief period where she actually believed she could see germs with the naked eye, right there on a spoon and the saltshaker and the kitchen sink sponge. But that episode passed, and it was like it never was.

Chapter 6

My Family History, According to Poppa

I've been told we come from tough stock. From Lithuania through Poland through Norway through Galveston, Texas, to West Virginia. Our people settled in North Fork, McDowell County, on the Tug River, right across from the Hatfields of the Hatfields and the McCoys. My great grandmother on Reuben Henry's side ran a kosher boarding house for Jewish salesmen down from the river towns like Wheeling, Cincinnati, Louisville, and Pittsburgh. Samuel Hermanson, Shlomochaim, my great grandfather, was a butcher, a gregarious man with a huge heart, but not to be trusted. Sam Hermanson disproved the myth that Jews were not drinkers. The town fathers got together and concocted a plan to burn down the town for the insurance money. They all pitched in on the policy but not Sam who thought they were bluffing.

The night of the fire, neighbors dragged Sam's equipment from the butcher shop out into the street. He was so drunk he could barely stand but not so drunk that he couldn't drag all his goods back inside where they burned to a crisp with everything else. Sam hopped a boxcar and disappeared. Katie Rose, his wife, wasn't worried. Apparently, he did this every so often, so she knew he'd be back. He always did. Rumor had it that Sam Hermanson fathered another child, a son, still down there somewhere in West "By God"

Virginia. I guess I've got a cousin somewhere in those hills. Many times removed, of course. Was there a Bar Mitzvah? A circumcision? Does he take communion? Celebrate Easter? Or what? Does he hate Jews? Does he even know? Would he care?

Sam had a good buddy named Chiel Shure - a pas de deux of mischief. The family all blamed Chiel for corrupting Sam, but Poppa said all Chiel did was poke what was already there. Sleight of hand was his MO. Poppa always laughed when he told me this story, which he did lots. One of my favorites. Sam and Chiel were out walking one day when they were set upon by robbers. They took off running into the woods for cover. Poppa dove over this fallen tree and lay down flat behind it. There wasn't much room left so Chiel climbed over the fallen trunk and dropped down on top of Sam. The robbers weren't five feet away, but they never saw Sam and Chiel, so they left. Sam had been scared but not as scared as Chiel whose bladder did neither of them a favor. He'd lost control and pissed on himself and Sam, right under him, got the run-off.

But the way Poppa told how they got to West Virginia in the first place was my favorite.

"Picture a small Jewish village, a shtetl, in Lithuania on the Russian border, the Pale as it was known. The Hermansons had been there for as long as anyone could remember. Pescha Hermanson and Misha Lazer married young, too young, and five weeks later they regretted it, but it took another five years for Misha Lazer to bolt, leaving her to milk the cows, tend the garden, feed the chickens, collect the eggs. Enough! She wanted him back. So, the family authorized your great grandfather to find him. Sam could find him nowhere in Lithuania but had a tip that Misha Lazer had crossed into Poland, Warsaw, a big city. Sam found him in a brothel. He must've gotten a tip. Why else would he go there? Would it help to know that 75% of the brothels in Warsaw prior to World War II were owned by Jews, and the women who worked there were not the kind of Jewish girls your mothers wanted you to marry. We have no reason to believe that Samuel dawdled.

The family joke was to yell out at random moments, "Gatkes on!" Which was what Sam had yelled to Misha Lazer when he found him. "Gatkes on!" Sam said as he threw Misha's boxer shorts at him, informing the surprised young man, "We're going home."

"Somehow Misha Lazer managed to evade Sam and disappear. But Sam tracked him down in Prague. Yep, another brothel. You'd think he'd have learned to cover his tracks by now, but Misha Lazer was not about to go back and be pecked to death. Little tiny pieces of him. Bit by bit 'til he was nothing at all. No way. Next stop Sweden. Next, Galveston, Texas. Next, Keystone, West Virginia. And that's where Sam, who had no proper soles left on his boots, told Misha Lazer, "I'm staying here. Go where you want."

Misha Lazer was worn out. He'd travelled hard. Lithuania was a long way away. He decided to stay, and the two of them went into the butcher business. Sam taught Misha Lazer what to do and how to do it, and their business thrived to the point where they could begin bringing their family over to America.

"Not Pescha," wailed Misha Lazer.

"Everybody but Pescha?" asked Sam.

"Yes. Everybody. Just not her. It's bad enough we'll both be on the same continent."

"The mishbacha will decide," said Sam. "It's not up to me.'"

And the next morning Misha Lazer was gone. No surprise. He'd hired a horse and wagon to take him somewhere north of Wheeling. Your great grandfather stayed put, and that's how all the Hermansons came to West Virginia. And that included Tante Pescha, who got a divorce and married a gentile, the manager of the one bank in town. There's even a little street in North Fork named Hermanson Way. They'd hear the occasional cracks like, "Jews are angels compared to Catholics", but mostly they got along with the neighbors."

Poppa never did talk that much about his own mother other than to tell me about the time his Drill Instructor at boot camp cornered him and demanded to know, "What're you doin' in my Marine Corps, turd?"

"Sir," Poppa shot back, "Sir, it's safer than being at home, Sir." He said it was as if a total eclipse crept across his DI's face and coated it with disgust. "Shit-for-Brains, get the fuck outta my sight," he spat.

One of the rare times he did talk about her, Poppa said being home was like being in a free fire zone laced with trip wires. An IED named *M-O-M* could detonate any time. You never knew when the explosion would come. When it did, she struck with whatever weapon was at hand. He said that once she split the top of a desk with a baseball bat intended for his head. He said she should've married Vlad the Impaler. I told him I had no idea who that was and he just laughed.

Chapter 7

You'd be Surprised at What the River has to Say

The last day of fishing season always came at the beginning of Fall, so we always fished then, even if it was only for that one day. Poppa was a bait fisherman—Cheese Whiz, popcorn, mini-marshmallows, as well as your standard assortment of worms, bugs, and flies, some of them rubber, some plastic. Fly fishermen would hate Poppa, and those who knew him did. He deemed them high and mighty hypocrites. They deemed him a low life. Catch 'n' Release was horseshit, according to him, a fancy way to feel righteous about what it was, which was to scare the shit out of a fish, take a picture, throw it back, and celebrate.

According to Poppa, that was so they could feel like they hadn't damaged nature, hadn't been cruel, hadn't upset the ecosystem. "Feel good, bub," he yelled at some of them like they could hear him downstream, "'Cause what you really did was panic a sentient being into believing it's going to die. You have fun while that poor creature fights for its life. It doesn't know you're playing. It thinks it's going to die, you shmuck! So, you unhook it and set it free. Hooray. Sometimes the fish is in such shock you need to scratch its belly to get it moving again. Poor fish has PTSD for the rest of its life. We both do the same thing 'cept I eat it, and you torture it. In the eyes of the Almighty, who wins?"

We have a wide and boisterous creek a few yards from our front door, an exquisite stretch of water with good holes to fish, not so many willow banks so roll casting is minimal. Easy stuff for beginners. The state designated our creek as a public fishing spot, yellow signs nailed to trees: Public Fishing. Folks with a lot of expensive equipment came to the small bridge in front of our house. Somehow those yellow signs disappeared overnight, replaced by other yellow signs stating no trespassing. The week-end fishermen disappeared, too. That lasted a good while, but, when the state finally found out about it, the rangers came banging on our front door. They knew Poppa, and they knew he did it, but Poppa denied it, and they couldn't prove it. "Blame Vogue magazine," Poppa said. Vogue had done a feature on our valley as a hidden paradise. Overnight it became a destination place for hikers and campers and leaf peepers and fishermen and hunters and bikers and runners. It was an invasion to us, and the locals, with the exception of the real estate crowd, who were not happy about it.

Dollar General bought an empty church in the village with plans to turn it into a store. It burned down overnight. Nobody knew how that could have happened. The volunteer fire department was practically opposite the church, but their door got stuck or something, so by the time they got their hoses out the place was cinders. A fellow from Brooklyn had plans to build a brewery in the middle of the village. He promised jobs and free beer. Didn't matter. He was threatened with death and dismemberment at a planning board meeting.

Poppa wrote Vogue asking that they retract the first story and publish another labelling our territory one of the most dangerous spots for tourists in these mountains. They did not, and the yellow signs went up again. Poppa needed a new tactic. On good fishing days, he'd carry a cooler filled with beer to the middle of the bridge, along with his spinning rod, a boombox, and a fresh batch of popcorn, he'd rig half a dozen or so lines off the bridge, bait the hooks with a flourish, drop the lines over the side then sit down on the boombox, slap in a Buddy Holly tape, drink beer, start singing along, and doze off. It was like a scarecrow in the garden. No birds got close. Word got around. The yellow signs stayed in place, but none of the fishermen did. *Good*, Poppa said. He could once again stand on the bridge listening to the creek just below. Water makes a different sound as it runs over each different stretch of its bed. Poppa was happy he could hear it again. I liked to listen with him. You'd be surprised at what the river has to say. It never says the same thing twice.

After that, one of the neighbors left a bottle of Maker's Mark on the front stoop as thanks, and Poppa got lots of winks and "Have-a-nice-days" down at the post office.

Mostly, Poppa's dealings with people were pretty good. He really didn't discriminate. He'd look at a huge and complex road building machine and admire the guy who made it as much as he admired Da Vinci.

"Some guy tinkering in his workshop thought that thing up, figured it out then made it, and it works, and you're telling me that's not as prodigious a thing as anything? Strength. Precision. I'd put that in a museum, too. Threshers. Combines. Dozers. Garbage trucks. Where'd we be without the garbage truck? Somebody real smart had to design them. Get *them* in the Smithsonian next to the Wright Brothers plane. Da Vinci created a flying machine but did his flying machine fly? He created a submarine, but did it work? Nope, not if he wanted to keep breathing, but that roadbuilder flattens mountains, and that garbage truck disappears our bilge, and that dozer goes where you point it. Nobody ever said this world was a fair one."

I asked him, "What about Michelangelo?", and he asked me, "What about totem poles?" Poppa always provided a new perspective.

Chapter 8

Then There Was Dub

Poppa had suffered that son-of-a-bitch Dub Tuttle long enough. His place was across the creek, our closest neighbor. Poppa's idea of being a good neighbor was to help out when needed, day, night, holidays, rain, shine, four feet of snow, hail, tornado, or heatwave, but you didn't need to be in his living room, and he didn't need to be in yours. Dub's idea of being neighborly meant telling you your grass needs cutting or your car is blocking his garbage bin. Dub would talk your ear off if you were in shouting distance. He'd begin by hollering but gradually closed the distance and lowered his voice until he was practically whispering in your ear.

Poppa said his holler sounded like a foghorn, his whisper like a gas leak, and his opinions were to the right of Attila the Hun. Although he was savvy enough, except for the occasional slip, not to foist them on us, but we knew what they were. To his credit, Dub did not keep a framed picture of Mussolini on his wall like Poppa joked he did. But he did give Hitler credit for making the trains run on time.

"What's fair is fair," Dub told Poppa, "Gotta give a man his due."

"He got his due when he put a bullet in his head." Then Poppa informed him that he'd been in Germany in 1938, working in Berlin. "There wasn't a train in sight when you wanted one."

"I heard different," said Dub.

"Were you there?"

"Why would I be?" cracked Dub.

"Sounds like your kind of place," said Poppa.

Later, Poppa told me he'd lied. He wasn't in Germany in 1938. He'd never been to Germany in his entire life, never wanted to, had no plans to go anywhere close, *wouldn't set foot in the goddamn place if their politburo gave me an all expense tour for Oktoberfest*. But what did Dub know? *A goddamn closet nazi zombie coyote scumbag son of a bitch*, according to Poppa.

Word got around that my Poppa, Reuben Henry, had a great bird dog, a lab named Buster aka Buster Fleabag according to Aunt Gert. Poppa explained to me how bird dogs like springer spaniels and Brittany spaniels quartered back and forth at a good clip. Buster was methodical. He poked along with one thing on his mind: Bird. He didn't know how to do anything else besides sleep and eat. What he'd do was stand in front of a closed door and just stare at it. Aunt Gert mocked him in a slow, goofy voice. "Do I go through it or around it or just stand here forever? I'm gonna just stand here forever. Or what? Huh?"

If there was but one bird within a mile, Buster would find it. Poppa said his perseverance slowed him down, every blade of grass, every fallen twig. He'd plod through brush at his own slow pace, pick up the scent, follow it to its rightful owner, at which point, the bird flushed, and Poppa got it. Buster flushed. Poppa shot. *A bird in the bag. A bird in the pot*. The perfect team. They knew each other well.

Poppa got Buster as a pup, although this was now years later. It had been a choice between two retrievers, Labrador, and a Chesapeake Bay. Both he said were superb dogs, but with totally different temperaments. "If you've got a Chessie with you in your duck blind when the warden comes to check your limit, the Chessie'll take his arm off, but, if you've got a Lab in your blind, your baby will wag its tail and happily show the warden where the ducks are stashed. Poppa's choice - a black Lab with a big head and a small brain – our Buster. They were suited for each other. Poppa'd rather shake your hand than bite it.

I overheard Poppa tell someone that he preferred hunting with Buster to seventy virgins in paradise. Regardless of IQ and number of legs, when they were in the field, Poppa and Buster were one. Not a word, not a bark passed between them. Poppa would think it and it would happen. Buster would lie around all day barely twitching a single muscle to flick a fly, but   as soon as Poppa went to the gun closet and took out the bell Buster wore around his neck, Buster was like a puppy all over again. Poppa loved it when the only sound he heard was Buster's bell as he moved through high grass. Couldn't see Buster, but that bell...*clong clong clong...a dull clong clong clong...*

Poppa always knew where Buster was and what was in front of him. He didn't point. He flushed. He chased it down. He rumbled like a tank. A cluck and a squawk and a drumming of wings and a rocket bursting into the air from dense cover, the thunder being different depending on whether the bird was a pheasant or grouse. A pheasant cackles and flushes and heads for the hills. A grouse thunders, veers, and vanishes.

Poppa loved to talk about the best day he and Buster ever had in all their days when all they'd done was sit underneath a wild apple tree the whole livelong day, thirty- two degrees at dawn, sixty-five at dusk, and a gentle drizzle. Normally, Poppa said Buster kept his distance at about five yards. But that day he put his big, square, dumb head in Poppa's lap and kept it there. Buster loved to have the inside of his ears scratched. Poppa would scratch his own back against the trunk of the tree, up and down and a shiver between the shoulders, like a bear.

Another day he told me about, one where communication was only by thought. Poppa said he and Buster were not two different species that day but something other only they could be and know.

"Sunlight filtered down through a low-lying fog, in some places revealing the ground spackled with the random growth of that cover. It was like we'd discovered this world as we moved through it—infinitely more beautiful than anything they'd experienced before. We were sauntering through an enchanted land. There'd been an overnight freeze, so the ground crackled step upon step. Chiarascuro cracked rocks into fractals and twisted branches into garlands. Buster lurched forward, dropped his head, and lunged like a fullback on the one. A gaudy pheasant broke from the mist and made for the sky. I fired. The bird goes down, touches down, but immediately swoops back up because all I'd done was ding it. Up it went but so did Buster— three feet, nearly four—snatched that bird right out of the air. No major league center fielder could've done it any better, but it came with a look of utter disdain from Buster. Poppa smiled when he gave me his best Buster imitation, "You blew it," Buster would have said if he could have said it, "I bailed your ass out, turkey. Forget the braggin' rights on this one."

When Dub heard about Buster, he had to see for himself. Dub had pheasant on his property, so he invited Poppa and Buster to come try their luck.

"What's the lucky part, Dub?" asked Poppa.

"You're here, aintcha?" Dub snapped back.

Buster lived up to his reputation. Three pheasant up. Three pheasant down. Poppa gave him his head. The first thing Buster did was walk the perimeter of the field. At one end, Buster waddled through a section of swale so wide and thick Poppa wondered if it'd ever end. Didn't bother Buster a bit. He plodded on in his own slowpoke way. Of course, that's where the birds were hiding, smack in the middle of that boggy fortress, only Buster flushed them, found them, and brought them back. Dub's mouth hung open. He was salivating. *Looked like he had rabies*, quipped Poppa.

Some days later, Dub calls to say he's coming over. Which was unusual. But he wanted to show Poppa what he'd gotten—a puppy—a cute little Brittany spaniel.

"I'm gonna train him 'til he out hunts yours," said Dub, always subtle.

"Nice looking pup," said Poppa, "Best of luck."

"He's a tiger," said Dub.

"Save some birds for me, will ya, Dub?"

Weeks went by. No Dub, not until he showed up at the front door uninvited and smiling like a pumpkin.

"Reuben Henry," he said, "Buster's met his match."

"I didn't think this was a contest," said Poppa.

"Everything is," said Dub. "Where you been?"

The plan was to hunt first thing.

Once Dub was out the door, Poppa's tone got real serious. "Listen to me, Thea. You can insult a man's wife. Insult his kids, his car, his special bar-b-q sauce, but don't you never ever criticize a man's hunting dog. It is a sacred creature, and blaspheming God's Own will surely get you hurt if not mutilated and killed."

That said,

Poppa takes Buster over to Dub's place and takes me with him. Dub's got his Brittany with him, gloating until he sees me.

"What's she doin' here?"

"I can't seem to get rid of her," Poppa said with a smile, letting me know he was only fooling.

"Ain't right," groused Dub.

"Where's it written?" asked Poppa.

"It don't need to be written," Dub said back, "It is what it is."

"It is what it *was*," said Poppa. "C'mon, let's hunt. You stay behind me, Thea."

"Mitzi's gonna tear Buster a new one."

"So be it," said Poppa.

They separated maybe fifteen feet and began to work the field. It hadn't been tilled for who knows how long, so chunks of scraggly brush pocked the place. Paradise if you happened to be a pheasant. Buster's plodding along. Mitzi sprints back and forth—she puts one up—it's almost out of range. Dub's a pretty fair shot himself, didn't miss much. He didn't that time, either. As the bird plummeted towards earth, Dub gloated, like a dad with a newborn handing out cheap cigars. It was, I thought, the world's most disgusting smirk on his fat, smug face. He absolutely loved himself at this moment.

"Mitzi, huh?" he said to Poppa.

"Mitzi, huh," Poppa said, pointing with his chin.

Mitzi was standing over the bird.

"Bring it here, good girl," said Dub, rightfully expecting his expensive retriever to retrieve. "That's a good girl. Bring it to daddy."

Mitzi took the bird in her mouth, looked hard at Dub, turned, ran in the opposite direction, and buried it. Buried it! Dug a hole and dropped it in. Plop. Every time Dub got a bird, Mitzi would run away and bury it. She was so proud of herself. It was then that I got what Poppa meant. You don't laugh at such a thing.

Dub was apoplectic. Had we even chuckled, he would've shot us both dead. Instead, he shot Mitzi, and even *that* wasn't the worst thing about him. Here's what was.

Dub had two grown sons who worked in the city but spent every second of their free time at his place. *Their* place, actually, as it would be passed down to them after their father's death. They grew up there, fished and hunted, split wood, helped put a new roof on the barn, planted trees, tended a garden. The place was home. Their home. But they had no clue.

Decades past, Dub got a divorce from the boys' mother, only the boys took their mother's side, planting a grudge deep in Dub's heart that festered over the years. He spent a lifetime plotting his revenge. Against his own sons. They had no idea. Dub took up with a woman the last two years of his life. I think her name was Bessie, maybe, Bertha, something with a "B". Poppa wasn't sure. Dub left his entire place to her. Dub did. Cut his kids right out of the will, out of every damn thing they should've had coming to them. She later sold it for close to a million dollars. She seemed like a nice person, but, come on, who does that to their kids? Not that Dub's boys weren't also mini-Dubs, especially the youngest, a genuine hard-off if ever there was one. Harley—Poppa said Harley only had one expression—dumb.

After Dub shot that sweet dog of his, we didn't see him for a while.

Chapter 9

The Tuttles, the Worst of the Worst

Locals were mindful of Floyd & Lloyd, how they lived their lives with a wink and a nudge. Never hurt no one. They were local fixtures, born here, and only a death away from local legend. Nobody put Harley Tuttle in the same category. Mostly, they put him in the category of "Little Prick." Beer was Harley's favorite food. The guy was arrested for shoplifting pretzels at the Quik Chek in Tannersville, was nailed for driving 95 in a 25-mph zone. Anybody asked him to help do something he usually wouldn't, or he might do it half-ass if it paid and he needed the money. Farts were a whole way of life with Harley. I heard he was suspended from high school for farting during class on purpose. When he got a little older, he was made to sit in the last row closest to the door at town meetings (most of which he and his father didn't attend).

Until the Hmongs came to our valley.

They were refugees from Vietnam who'd fought with American soldiers against Ho Chi Min. Poppa told me the patriarch of their clan lost a hand and an eye while defusing a booby-trap. His wife, a mother, risked her life daily by shuttling messages back and forth. Their children kept eyes out for the enemy. One of the reasons the State Department placed them in our valley was because they were excellent farmers. The state had sponsored them, giving them tillable land, including pasture enough for two horses and a donkey, and a fix-er-up house just north of our valley. The family planned to develop their place into a thriving business—farm stand, maple syrup, smoked fish, pumpkins, alpacas, the promise of tomatoes big as pomegranates, sugar sweet peas, lamb's ear, and purple echinacea. Some folks acted unfriendly, suspicious, but most in our village welcomed the Hmong family as their own.

Not Dub Tuttle.

"Before we re-zone this parcel, how do we know we want these people here? Sounds like 40 goddamn acres and a mule."

I sat anxiously in that town meeting next to Papa waiting for an explosion.

"What's your beef?" Poppa asked him.

"Got no beef, *neighbor*, none at all. Just lookin' out for the neighborhood. Real estate values mean something. This is a quiet community. We don't want no zombies in our front yards—don't want no chickens and goats slaughtered in the park. They stick jellybeans on toothpicks and shove 'em up nostrils to decorate the carcass. Ever hear their music? Ever smell one of 'em? They come from a shithole country."

"They come from Vietnam, Dub," said Poppa.

"Slope City."

"Hmong tribesmen, Dub. They fought side by side with our special forces. The old man, the patriarch of their clan, lost an eye and a hand defusing an anti-personnel mine."

"Can't dispute one word you say, but what I'm askin' here is, are these people free of disease? Were their clothes disinfected? *Were they*? Where they gonna work? Do they have a criminal record?"

"Your *son* has a criminal record, Tuttle! Breaking and entering, assault and battery, DUI—"

"My son ain't in this, Hermanson. *You* people would let *anybody* in."

"Sure as hell wouldn't let you in. What people?"

"You know who you are, and we know what you're doin'."

"We?"

"We."

"Well, 'we' know what you're doing, too."

"What's that?"

"Can you spell ignoramus? I doubt it. I vote to re-zone!"

"Ever seen their goddamn dogs? Fatheads. Barrel bodies. Face ugly enough to make you shit your pants."

"Buy a diaper. Walmart's having a sale. Don't forget the wipes."

The town planning board voted to rezone, and the Hmong family was welcomed with a bake sale from the local ladies' auxiliary and a chicken bar-b-que sponsored by the fire department.

Poppa told me he and Dub Tuttle didn't say a word to each other for months after that, not until hunting season. We all knew there were some folks who agreed with Dub, but they didn't like the way he drove top speed and drunk up and down the valley, broken muffler, ear splitting and proud of it, so the hell with him.

One Saturday morning in the kitchen, I was maybe seventeen at the time, Poppa told me about a dream he'd had the night before starring Dub Tuttle. Poppa prided himself on being able to discuss tractors, pick-ups, and bullet trajectories as well as any local, often at the American Legion over chicken wings and a cold Bud. He could talk a good game with the university crowd as well. Aristotle, Watson & Crick, Edna St. Vincent Millay, quantum physics (well, sort of, and I can bullshit what I don't know, he admitted), even chaos theory. Actually, Poppa could talk to pretty much anybody. Much to the bane of my existence, he taught me how to talk to anyone as well. He could talk, and so could I, not always to our advantage since we always said what we thought while couching our opinions in the nicest possible way. The trick was to state your beliefs and opinions without using your words as a bludgeon. "*Smile when you say that,*" Poppa told me, quoting some actor from a gangster movie.

In his dream, Dub and Poppa are standing at the Legion bar. Dub said something to him, ignorant as usual. Papa couldn't remember exactly—Dub said so many asinine things about Blacks, Hispanics, traitors (of which Poppa was one, the leader of a cabal), women, Jews, Catholics, democrats, welfare queens, and queens, period. (Dub favored the expression, "Light in the loafers"), which was funny considering Poppa told me Dub was once arrested for soliciting sex in a men's bathroom at Reagan International. "He claimed he had a wide stance, so nothing happened to him. Then I woke up."

"You woke up."

"I woke up."

"That's it?"

"I skipped the part where I killed him."

"Too bad"

"Win a few. Lose a few."

"What's a zombie coyote?"

"A zombie coyote's somebody who looks harmless but isn't. He's all bullshit, but it's dangerous bullshit, slimy bullshit, don't turn your back bullshit. Dub worked for the gas and electric company. Ever see his basement? Ladders, tools, generators, all kinds of equipment, every piece stolen from work."

"I always wondered why you never went after him."

"And do what?"

"Slash his tires. Pour sugar in his gas tank. Sprinkle deer feed on his roses. I can think of a lot of stuff. Jesus, Poppa, they killed Buster."

"And Harley killed himself. Caught his wife with another guy on their new shag carpet, ran into the bedroom, and shot himself. Nobody should lose a kid like that, even if the kid is an evil prick which we all know he was. I didn't have to go after Dub. Outta my hands. I'm not sorry for the man. The wheel turned and he got run over.

Poppa was used to letting Buster roam free. One neighbor, about a quarter mile down the valley, was a baker who brought his stale sweet buns back here for the deer to eat. Buster made two trips a day. Mornings he'd ramble early, visit Kelly, his girlfriend, a chocolate Lab who ruled the baker's roost, eat a few stale buns, take a dip in the pond with Kelly, then roam off on his own. Evenings, who knows where he went? It was Buster's secret. Come hunting season, Poppa always made certain Buster wore an orange vest, kept him from being shot, although some arcane law stated that if someone saw a dog chasing a deer, they could shoot the dog. Buster was too old, then, to chase anything, but come morning when he hadn't come back, Poppa and I went out to look for him. We crossed and quartered Dub's field into the woods beyond, *cutting for sign*. Poppa told me they say that in Montana. We walked through the woods for hours. Buster had to be somewhere.

We came to a ridge thick with mountain laurel and there he was under the bush where he'd dragged himself to die after being shot and killed by a bolt from a crossbow that tore through his orange vest and took out his heart. Sobbing, I dropped to my knees next to our Buster. Poppa placed his shaky hand on my shoulder, a broken sound escaping him.

We both knew the only person who had a crossbow was Dub's idiot son Harley. So that's where we went. Poppa cradled Buster in his arms and carried him all the way to Dub's place. I gotta admit I was scared, but Poppa was determined, and I wasn't about to let him go there alone. If they did do something to him, they'd have to do something to me, too.

Poppa stood out front Dub Tuttle's house and bellowed, "Dub Tuttle!"

Standing beside him, furious, my heart raced.

Poppa bellowed again. This time Dub came out to the porch. He looked at dead Buster in Poppa's arms.

"Somebody shot him."

"My sympathies."

"With a crossbow," Poppa said.

"What's that got to do with me?"

"Nothing."

"So why're ya here?"

"Would you ask your son to come out here?" asked Poppa.

"Which one?"

"The dumb one."

"My oldest dumb one or my youngest dumb one?

"The one with a crossbow."

"So what?" said Dub.

"So, I'd like to talk with him," said Poppa.

"Lemme give you some heartfelt advice," offered Dub. "Don't piss him off. He's got problems. Anger stuff. Issues. Marine raiders kicked him out on a section eight. Just sayin'. As a friend." He cleared his throat and spit off the porch.

"Harley," Dub hollered, "Get your fat ass out here! Man wants to see you."

Harley shuffled out to the porch holding a can of spiked lemonade. He'd gotten fat since the Corps kicked him out.

Harley belched. "What's up?"

Poppa held Buster out for Harley to see. Harley seemed unfazed.

"He was chasing a deer," Harley said flatly.

"You're a goddamn liar."

Oh, shit, I thought, even though I was glad he'd said it.

Harley's eyes got small, his cheeks turned red, and he cracked his knuckles.

"It's the law," growled Harley.

As mad as I'd ever seen him, Poppa handed Buster to me, then looked up at Harley.

"And I said you're a liar."

"Can't say you weren't warned," Dub called out as Harley, his face blood-red, started for Poppa, fists clenched, beady eyes locked on target.

Poppa wasn't fazed. He held his hands up.

"Hold on there, Harley."

Harley stopped halfway to Poppa.

"I'm an old man, Harley. Whatcha gonna do?"

"Old enough to die."

"We all die, Einstein. Now here's the way I see it. You've got three choices. First off, you can beat the living shit out of me, which will most definitely get you thrown in jail, maybe even prison, and brand you forever after as the pussy who beat up an old man after shooting his best friend. Second choice, I beat the shit out of you."

"Not gonna happen."

"We're talking hypothetical, of course. You know what hypothetical means, Harley?"

"You ain't shit," spit Harley, some of it dribbling down his chin.

"To continue. Choice number two. I beat the crap out of you. Drop you in your tracks. Something sneaky you don't expect. Kidney. Gonads. Whatever. Muscle memory takes over. Whop! Whop! Think about your reputation, Harley. Think of those jokers at the Legion, Harley. You're gonna get pissed on and laughed at. An old man beat you. You never know."

"What's choice number three?"

"There is no choice number three. I lied."

"I could rip you apart," Harley threatened, but he looked nervous.

"Your call," Poppa said.

I set Buster down gently, in awe of how my Poppa kept his cool. I had to get into this.

"Hey, murderer, you're gonna have to beat up a girl, too, 'cause if you touch my Poppa, at some point I'm gonna come up behind you and bust your skull like a watermelon." There was a good thick stick the size of a baseball bat on the lawn, I went over and picked it up. "This'll do."

Harley smirked. "You ain't shit, little girl."

"Try me," I said, holding that branch and giving him a look like I meant to kill.

"Go on, try her," said Poppa.

"Two of you ain't worth shit," he sputtered.

"Get the hell off my property before you all get hurt," ordered Dub.

"Me, too?" I said.

"Shut the fuck up," shouted Dub.

"You shut the fuck up!" I screamed back at him. "And tell that brain damaged bad seed of yours you call a human that if he so much as touches my Poppa, I'll hire someone to kill him if I can't do it myself."

"You know Officer Colby?" asked Poppa. "State trooper? *Good* friend of mine. I'll send him on over once we get home."

Poppa picked up Buster and we walked away, both of us wishing we could have mangled Harley, frustrated we couldn't. Wasn't worth jail time.

We buried Buster in the apple orchard. It was our favorite place to just hang. I'd eat an apple, and he'd always eat the core. After, when we were standing side-by-side at Buster's grave, my heart broke when I saw Poppa was crying. It was the only time I ever remember seeing him cry.

Chapter 10

A Truck Stop

My neck hurt. My back ached. The road was beginning to blur. I wanted to get there, but I wanted to get there alive. Coffee. Apple pie. Adderall. A bathroom. Some deluded being had left a small booklet, maybe two inches by four inches, on the toilet seat. *THIS WAS YOUR LIFE*. A kind of comic book with sketches of poor souls going to Hell. Death? Nothing to be afraid of. You can be saved. Don't sweat it. I'm sure whoever did this was certain they were saving a soul. *Jesus saves. Moses invests.* Where'd I hear that one?

Pass.

When Poppa was a kid, he said the two by four was a considerably different kind of beast–a porno comic strip of those dimensions printed on cheap paper with popular cartoon characters sketched in black and white–like Blondie & Dagwood (doggy style), Mickey & Minnie (bondage), Bugs Bunny & Elmer Fudd (your guess) ...All these creatures doin' it with gusto every whichaway and then some. Portia Pig and Goofy? You got the picture. Pictures. Worth a fortune on eBay. Sometimes I think the inside of my head is like a junk shop where everything's on consignment. I'm always surprised at what's in it.

The coffee and Adderall hadn't yet kicked in, so I decided to roll a big fatty, put my head back, close my eyes, and rest a bit before my last leg.

I've never married, got nothing against it–I think it'd be nice waking up with the same warm body every morning–but I sometimes wonder…I don't know…I just wonder… I do have a new friend whom I now see. He's not at all perfect, but neither is anyone else. Most, less so. He worked his way through med school selling hot dogs from a pushcart. Poppa met him. They got along gangbusters. Both of them had great stories to tell and kept each other howling. I don't know. Poppa told his favorite, one about Floyd and Lloyd, one I hadn't heard for a long time– these Catskill waters were the home of fly fishing in America. Floyd and Lloyd were well known fishing guides. Fly fishermen from all over came to fish with them. Even British royalty sought their services–The Duke of Windsor and the Earl of Leicester. The two royals flew into Albany then drove south through the Hudson Valley to the banks of the Esopus near Edgar Shoemaker's old dairy barn. They met the twins at a good-sized shack where one could put their feet up, taste the applejack, talk fishing. Introductions all around. The Duke of Windsor and the Earl of Leicester were quite gracious as all hands were being pumped, Floyd, the more outgoing of the two, smiled his best and biggest smile when he stuck out his hand and said, "Howdy, Duke. Howdy, Earl. We got some big ones waitin' on ya." Howdy, Duke! Howdy, Earl! Duke 'n' Earl! You believe that? True story, he said. They're still howling at Buckingham Palace. Poppa always lost it at his own punchline.

Once, the two brothers were interviewed for an article in a local paper. When asked by the reporter what changes had they seen over the many years they've lived here, they stood there and thought for a while. Then stood and thought some more. Then Floyd nudged Lloyd who answered, "They's less cows."

Poppa said they were fixtures, history, as much a part of these mountains as any of its critters. Literally, they cruised up and down the valley twice daily in an ancient Ford pick-up, top speed fifteen miles per hour, more often ten. These guys knew every landmark in the valley - where each well was first dug, where the first big dish tv antenna was set, where Buddy Berger got his ten pointer, where the dump truck full of gravel missed its turn and went off the bridge, the spot where Edna's great uncle shot himself, where the goats ate the roses. There was a time when suicide among farmers was common when the man came to consider himself unable to work anymore, useless. They reminded us of a time gone by when things seemed easier, not so much a reminder because we weren't there to remember in the first place. And, anyway, it wasn't, but, still, Lloyd and Floyd sanctified the myth. They lived the life they were handed. It was what they knew, made do, enjoyed, and yearned for no other. They kept a field in hay and worked a substantial garden, fixed their own equipment, stilled their own whiskey, and poached their meat, like Robin Hood in Sherwood Forest. The idea of a "forest bath" would have struck these two old fuckers as incomprehensible, especially since these guys were in the woods most every day but only bathed once a week. Sometimes. Maybe. They migrated east from the Irish Alps in northern Greene County. If Olympic medals were given out for the amount of whiskey consumed on any given day, they'd get gold. The brothers swore that they weren't drunk as long as they could hold on while lying down. You could normally find a deer carcass hanging in the barn. They swore on the Bible that it tripped and broke its leg jumping over their fence.

They'd known my grandmother Sophie Rose's family for generations and were there to watch her grow up. Her local roots went deep. The first deed was in 1820. Its foundation, the original, was stone stacked by hand. When she and my Poppa moved in, Floyd and Lloyd took it upon themselves to "adopt" them. First thing, they gave a pig roast for the new folks, and invited the entire valley. They supplied the pig and whiskey. Everyone else brought the rest: ambrosia, slaw, brownies, mac and cheese. When Floyd and Lloyd came down with the flu, Poppa and my grandma were there. The boys were lapsed Catholics, but they relied on some force from somewhere which told them to refuse medication. When my grandma looked in their medicine chest, all she found was a bottle of aspirin and a bottle of holy water. The seal on the aspirin bottle was still intact. The bottle of holy water was nearly empty. Floyd and Lloyd requested a quart of apple jack and said, don't worry, they'd be just fine. And they were.

When Lloyd died, Floyd died. Then there was an emptiness in the valley.

I was a month old when Poppa first held me and took me home, the only one I've ever had. My profession keeps me away for months at a time. I know Aunt Gertie's back there keeping both eyes on him. He's still a rascal who can yank your chain, but last time I saw him, before I went to Alaska, he had begun to weaken. That fall didn't help. Took it late one night with no memory of how, got out of bed at three a.m. to tap his bladder, and all of a sudden, walking to the john, no warning, he found himself falling to the floor. He'd been trained how to fall in the Marine Corps, sixty years ago, and still had enough presence of mind to slightly twist his body so he'd hit in a better position. Nothing broke, but his head slammed against the floor so hard he really thought he might die. Good thing it was carpet and not bare wood.   He hadn't tripped. He hadn't stumbled. He hadn't slipped. It wasn't a stroke. It was a surprise fall, although what fall isn't a surprise? Poppa lay on the floor until he felt strong enough to stand. No wobble. Balance intact.

At first, he told nobody, but an annoying headache persisted, so he told me. I took him to the emergency room where he had a CT scan that revealed no damage. Fine. No problem. Let's go home. Poppa went about his normal business for the next four months, maybe a bit off balance, slight memory problem, but really OK. Then, one morning Poppa skipped breakfast, his favorite meal: biscuits and gravy, shrimp 'n' grits, shit on a shingle–choose one. "Take me now, Lord. Take me now," he'd say at every first bite. I went to his room, knocked, got no response, called, no response, opened the door. Poppa was on the floor writhing and flailing about as if his limbs were the limbs of rag dolls. His eyes had rolled back in his head. Noises of a beast grunted deep down his gut. Scariest thing I'd ever seen, and remember, I'm a nurse. I don't spook. But he was Reuben Henry. He was Poppa. Poppa.

Paramedics came, and we got him to the hospital. He was in and out with no idea what had happened, no idea where he was going, no idea why. What he remembered and all he remembered was an attractive neurosurgeon in her white coat and heels. Heels! Red ones! No lie. "I was still alive," he later remarked. Diagnosis: subdural hematoma. Poppa could have died. A weaker man would have. The staff gasped in disbelief when they learned his age. He looked twenty years younger. The staff said Poppa was the strongest, most energetic patient they'd seen at his age and younger. Blood on the brain. He'd been bleeding for four months since his fall without knowing it. Minor stuff. A bit of imbalance. Minor memory lapses. Nothing much except the pressure built and built until it caused the seizure.

Seizures.

Instead of dying, he spent a week in the hospital and healed in record time. Except for his absolute refusal to "do his business" on a commode in the corner of his room, insisting on the bathroom with the door locked, he was the floor's favorite patient. He sent out for Thai food one day, sushi the next. Even when he was released his activities were restricted: no driving for twelve months, no alcohol, not even one lonely single can of light beer, use a cane, don't lift more than five pounds, don't stare at a screen or read for too long. There were more. Who remembers? Use a walker? He'd rather die. Poppa still wanted to do what he wanted to do. He didn't drive, but only because he risked jail time if caught within a year of his seizures. That left everything else.

"Life's too short," he told me.

"You're going to make it shorter," I shot back.

"Mais, où sont les neiges d'an temp?"

"Huh?"

"Where are the snows of yesteryear? In French."

"What's that got to do with anything, Reuben Henry?"

"It does, and it doesn't."

"Huh?"

"I think therefore I am." Descarte."

"I know who it is." I said.

"Don't get testy," said Poppa." I'm an old man."

"Some excuse," I snapped.

Poppa was home recuperating when I got a call that a close friend had just been diagnosed with a brain tumor and probably wouldn't live out the week.

A neighbor stayed with Poppa so I could hurry to the hospice where she'd been admitted. We prayed and sang and cried, hugged each other as she died. It was an intense and profound experience, one that has never left me. There are things I call on, things which get me through. When I got home, I told Poppa about my week, how important it was. He listened respectfully then said, "When my time comes, please, child, no prayers, no songs, no tears."

"That doesn't leave much."

"It leaves the colonel, Miss Lady," he said with a sly wink.

"What colonel?"

"You'll find him on the corner. When my time comes, just bring me a bucket of fried chicken."

"Fries?"

"Onion rings."

"Vanilla shake?"

"Large."

"Extra thick?"

"Now, we're talkin'," said Poppa.

*

He never said it, but I believe he felt this fall was an eye opener, the first time he knew he was old. Age had never meant anything to Poppa. He could talk to anybody. Three years old, thirty years old, ninety years old - didn't matter - but now it did. He didn't look it. He didn't act it. He didn't feel it at all, but he was - it - old - and Poppa was finally forced to confront it tooth and nail. He had been mother and father to me for so long I had trouble accepting it as well.

"Jesus Christ, Thea, get that look off your face. I'm still here. Got no plans to go anywhere."

"Want to make God laugh, tell Him your plans."

"I don't believe in God, so I'm safe. By the way, come up with

something original next time."

"You can argue with God and win, you know."

"Where'd you get that one?"

"Where do you think? From you! Hypothetical. If you did argue with God, *hypothetical*, what would you say?"

Silence my soul. These trees are prayers. I asked the tree, "Tell me about God", then it blossomed.

"I wish I'd written that. Years ago, there was this study to see if folks really had souls. What they did was weigh the corpse-to-be before death then weigh it again immediately after death to see if the soul left the body. After death, the body weighed a fraction less than before."

"Proving what?"

"My point exactly. Nothing but horse pucky. Obviously, folks need it. I respect their needs by keeping my pagan mouth shut. *T'ain't easy, MgGee.*"

*

I could see it now–his right hand trembled, not much, barely discernible– but enough for him to avoid ordering soup in a restaurant. His gait was a bit slower, balance just a tad off, less stamina, lids of jars were tighter than before, but his senses were intact, and his mind remained a wonder to me. He remembered all his passwords, but not where he parked his truck. Once was enough. "Should be a Goddamn ride at Disneyland." He talked his doctor into giving him a disabled parking sticker so he could park any damn place he wanted, maybe not in front of a firehouse or an emergency ward, but damn near anywhere else that pleased him.

On the Road Again, Last Lap

Your perspective changes. His did. Mine did.

When I was in school," Poppa said, "We'd read about these people who never left the place where they were born, never even ventured further than five miles from home. These folks had no need. Imagine that. No need. I could not fathom how any human being did not want to go further than five miles from home, but now I can. There's so much to do, too much, really. Got to check out the aphids on the roses, the monarchs on the milkweed, fisher tracks in deep snow, pumpkins in the Fall, apples in August, turkey season, deer season, small game, fruits and vegetables to put by, good books, brandy, fire in the hearth, Mozart playing, Stevie Nicks, Davis, Coltrane, Kenny Rogers–it's nonstop around here. Time to smell the sweet evening air. No need to worry about gridlock. Go where? Why? I might miss something."

Out of nowhere, he said one evening, "Mendacity. It's all mendacity. Tennessee Williams made those words come outta Big Daddy's mouth, and it's true. *Cat On a Hot Tin Roof... "* He smiled slyly and tapped his forehead, "'I coulda been a contender'. Brando, huh? The old brain. Still tickin'. I know you don't want it but I could do a speech from Coriolanus in a New York minute, if you wanted, which you probably don't."

"Correct."

"Here's what's really stupid. They sell you these drugs on TV to make you pee, to make you stop, to *shtup* your *nafka,* to juke your heart, to spike your brain, to ease your tuchos, to soften your bupkus, to shrink your kishkes, to tone your polkies–they tell you all the good stuff this drug's gonna do for you and that drug's gonna do for you, which is that it will treat this one thing wrong with you (consult your doctor; beg for a prescription; no guarantee). Then a serious, really boring, one note voice drones on in the background to tell you the dozens of things that can kill you or maim you or otherwise seriously mess you up while pretty music plays and people smile and drink umbrella drinks. Prostitution by another name. Pay me, and I'll say what you want. Money talks. Nobody walks." I no longer care whether or not I belong to this world because I don't belong to this world. Not my doing. Blame Darwin. No amount of effort to be with it will make me look like anything but a damned fool. *"I'm hip, dude."* Gag. See? I have nothing against it, find it curious, cruel, endless, and exasperating, but, yes, of course, compelling, too, but we're talking generations here, Toots, and these days, generations zoom by at supercalifragilistic speeds. And I really do not care because there's still so much to deal with as it is, so much I'm still trying to decipher. I thought I'd have the answers by now. Some answers. A few. At least, one? Nope. Uh, uh. Not yet unless you've got one hidden somewhere. I can't miss what I don't know. I can't aspire to dreams I've never had. I ride horses, not rocket ships. I eat meat more than once a week. I still have trouble with guys holding hands, but I'm working on it and have made considerable progress. Sue me. Necessity the mother of invention? Uh, uh. Invention's the mother of necessity. Did we really need a FAX machine? Other way around, Toots. Make something up then bullshit us we all need it. How else y'gonna get your corn beef sandwich? Rhythms, speech, magazine covers, collective thoughts, memes–some, mine; most, not."

I don't think he was trying to convince me of anything one way or the other, just that he was where he was, and had been where he'd been. He didn't want so badly to be anywhere else anymore. Are calm and curious an oxymoron? I got it, and so did he: Poppa had a life before this one. I hadn't, and the time came when I needed to leave. When I graduated as a full-fledged registered nurse, Poppa gave me a special nurse's watch that could be read upside down when taking a pulse. It's inscription: *Travel the world and come back home.*

"You grow up in West Virginia like I did," he told me, "Your mantra is 'When can I blow this pop stand?' One of life's conundrums. When I matriculated at WVU nobody wore overalls and work boots. They wouldn't dare, never even considered it, even for Halloween. Miner's kids struggling for their piece of the pie might be excused for doing something nasty to phonies playing dress up. Count me in. To call West Virginia enlightened would be like, um, well, you wouldn't put a neanderthal in charge of a nuclear weapons system, would you? But my fellow students were hardscrabble kids desperate for that piece of pie. They worked extra jobs to eat. Some mined off hours. They took jobs that would be shunned by the lowest caste in India.

There were rumors that a few of the coeds went up to Wheeling on weekends to service the truckers. Unpleasant but not as unpleasant as six kids in seven years with a shithead pill-head two fisted unemployed puff pastry for a husband. No need to report their income. Room, board, books, these were not rumors."

Chapter 11

SEMPER FI

When it was reported to General Chesty Puller - rat bastard genius - that the Chinese had his Marines surrounded at Chosin Reservoir, he said, "Good. Now, we know where they are."

First to fight. Last to eat.

My father did it. My grandfather did it. His father did it. So, I did it. The first woman in the family to join the Corps. I wanted to be a combat medic so I endured three months of Parris Island then trained with a basic grunt unit. I worked to be one of them. I never wanted to use what I knew, but I knew I could. I learned to see with the eyes in the back of my head. I heard the buzz and silence of the world around me. I could smell a change in temperature. I laughed with a sniper in my outfit who told me that if I heard his shot, he wasn't aiming at me. At the time, I really thought that was funny. Think of it in context. I believed that if you absolutely resolutely definitely wanted something destroyed overnight...well...Aye, aye, Sir. Send in the Marines. I believed that to be so, and proud of it. Semper Fi. And we were. And I was.

My unit was shipped to the streets of Kabul. House to house. Too many nooks and crannies. They shoot at you and disappear. They plant explosives in narrow alleyways. Where do I put my feet? What can't I touch? Does that adorable five-year-old have a bomb strapped around her tiny chest? Is that old woman pointing them out to you or you out to them? A street fight. Death smack in my face. A house of horror, houses of horror. These people were trying to kill us, and so we hated them. We took a lot of fire. It pierced our armor-plated vehicles because their armament was deficient. When one grunt questioned being sent to war without the proper equipment, the secretary of defense retorted that you go to war with the army you've got. Um, wait a minute. We were the invaders. You could have waited to take the time to properly insure the safety of the men you are sending out to die for you. "We who are about to die salute you?" More like, "We who are about to die, fuck you."

Something had punched me hard.

Why would they do that?

Some things were not so funny anymore.

I began to question.

"You've got your grandma's genes," he wrote.

Poppa wrote me daily. Wherever I was stationed, mail call always had a letter for me. "Forever the optimist, she'd give her all with the best of intentions. She knew other people might not be the same. So what? Nobody else was Sophie Rose but Sophie Rose. So be it. Of course, your mother was no slouch either, just another breed of "no slouch". Your grandmother could sit still and stare at something or nothing for hours, as quiet inside as a chapel. Your mother had to be in the trenches, always the social worker, member of the school board, wherever she was needed. Her hobby was baking bread and leaving it in neighbors' mailboxes. Told a Goddamn good story, too, like her dad. Very funny lady. Ever since she was a baby. She calls me one day screaming with laughter. At the time, she was a social worker in the children's division. Emergency care.

'Poppa, sit down. Breathe. Y'gotta hear this.'

She can barely talk, she's laughing so hard. Then she tells me about this client she had just driven back to the state mental institution. The woman had simply walked away the day before. Her kids were in your mother's care. She wanted to make sure they were all right when she walked away. Nothing seditious about that. Your mother normally had a good sense of direction but this place was way far out in the boonies, so, oops, she thought, where the hell am I? Right turn. Right turn. Right turn. Left turn. Then her client, who's sitting right there next to her, pipes up with, "You lost, aintcha?" Who wants to admit such a thing, but there you are. Your mother had no choice.

"Yes," she said, "I, uh…"

"Why dontcha do what I did?"

"What's that?" asked your mother.

"Well," said the woman, "I took off all my clothes 'n' jump up 'n'

down on the hood of the car."

True story. Your mother could've been a stand up. Smiling came natural. She made the sun come up. How she and your father ever got along I'll never know, but they did. He was a good man, I admit, although his way of looking at the world was not often in sync with mine. Nor was it always in sync with hers, but he listened to her when she explained poverty was not a character flaw but the result of inequity. So, that was a win. He listened to her when she explained that Ayn Rand was a bottom feeder. There were a few others– she shamed him into voting for a democrat. I believe he was a peacekeeper at heart. I know you've seen the picture of your father holding you in his arms right after your birth. Have you ever seen such a smile? Look at mine when your mother was born. It was radiant. It made the sun come up."

*

I could have gone to Officer Candidate School at Quantico, but I'd never liked most officers, anyway, so why would I want to be one? I took my discharge and went home.

Next?

I went to work for the local hospital. They were thrilled to get me–local Mountaineer makes good, comes home–but I was bored shitless, which is where *Nurses Without Borders* comes in. Poppa brought it to mind, and it stayed there. Good idea. I chose where and when and came back when I was finished. In the meantime, I'd be doing something decent for people.

It was Fall and good to be back home, but time was limited as I'd be taking off for Zimbabwe before Christmas. Poppa and I spent our ritual final day of fishing season on the bridge listening to Buddy Holly and eating Cheetos. A family of minks scampered over the rocks below, swam where there were none, and disappeared through high grass and weeds. Even from up here I could see how thick their coats had gotten. The deer, too–their coats had grown darker and thicker. Blue jays were shrieking. Squirrels scurrying. Even now, the pumpkins, big, fat, orange pumpkins.

Our trees were still bright with color, although not much red this year as the maples stayed yellow instead of turning red as they normally do. Too much rain, no frost is what the weather pundits up here say. A brisk wind is forecast to carom around the valley sometime tonight which means that the trees will be bare come morning. The old saw about the weather in the mountains is true: "Wait five minutes. It'll change."

The bare trees, I must admit, have always fascinated me more than the others. Whatever the intelligence that twists and distorts these limbs with no discernible design, arbitrary growths, no sense to them at all, whatever that intelligence, design or haphazard, the whole presents as perfect. Certainly, the autumn colors are exquisite. Who could not find them mesmerizing? I remembered an exhibition of impressionist paintings at the

National Museum in D.C. where it seemed as if I were in one. Come summer, full grown trees proudly puff out their great, green chests. They take in the sun. So, there is beauty, and there is pride, but is there mystery? To gaze on a winter forest with an endless array of bare trees with all parts torqued and contorted into harmony and intention as if under a magician's spell - on and on they go on forever - and they may well be there forever. Eternity? Maybe. Some of it.

Winter has been stalking us for weeks. Get out the fleece, flannel, and cleats. At least, the ticks will hibernate, and there won't be any tiny pests dive-bombing your inner ear.

Right now, nearing November, it seems quiet out there, but the house is ready - cracks are caulked, generators are charged, wood split and stacked, primed lanterns in every room - as if any of us are truly ready for one hundred and eighty straight days of snow and cold. And yet. Have you ever seen the full moon over a bed of fresh snow? The quiet beauty lowers one's blood pressure. No guilt. No worries. No fear. No nothin'. Poppa loved to quote the late, great Jackie Gleason, "How sweet it is!"

There is a rub. Always is, right? This time of year, things are unpredictable. A two-hundred-pound stag with a ten-point rack can suddenly stampede out of the brush and total your car. It happened to Poppa on Rte. 28 one night driving home. All he remembered seeing were antlers aligned with the hood ornament. That's all. Antlers. Big, thick beams. Whump! He said it was like Babe Ruth smacking a mattress with his Louisville Slugger. Bumper to solid flesh. A direct hit. A jolt from nowhere that totaled his car, killed the deer, and luckily didn't kill him. The power and placement of that hit sent that deer flying back over the roof. Poppa never saw it alive. Normally, things look smaller in death, but not this bruiser. He was a monster, one rarely seen and deeply desired, but he simply could not keep it in his pants, and it killed him.

A couple of days later, his car, still an accordion, Poppa was pulled over by a state trooper. "License and registration, please," he asked Poppa. Poppa wanted to know what he'd done. "License and registration, please," repeated the trooper, a bit more sternly. Poppa was irate but shouldn't have been. He failed to realize the trooper didn't need an excuse to ask for his ID. By the book. The trooper leaned in and snarled, "Have you got an attitude?"

"No," answered Poppa, "I'm too old to have an attitude."

*

It's the rut. Testosterone takes over rendering male deer stupid silly, not unlike fraternity brothers with a keg. Normally, this most cautious of animals is alert to every nuance of its environment. Not now. The only thing they want in life is a quick hook-up - names don't matter - and they will die to do it. Literally. Really, really die. There is no #MeToo movement in the local whitetail population. Does simply stand by while the bucks make fools of themselves until the biggest fool wins.

This means there is a great deal of death around here now. I don't mean hunting season where, agree with the activity or not, what is taken by locals is not wasted. The local hunters enter woods they've known since childhood with a great deal of knowledge, respect, and common sense. I'm talking about roadkill, an ugly word, loaded with disrespect and disdain for what was once a living, breathing creature of grace and beauty, too many of them beside roads that only a few years ago saw blissfully little traffic and now see too much, thanks to our valley being labelled "a destination place" in expensive magazines. More often you don't see the torn flesh, just the body lying there. You are not close enough and you are not likely to stop long enough to see the glazed eyes, the limp tongue. It could be asleep. These are the ones I wonder about.

"The question is not can they reason, or can they think, but can they suffer?" Jeremy Bentham, British philosopher, by way of Poppa, American Original.

I wonder about those that lie by the side of the road not yet dead but dying. Do they know they are dying? We do. We who walk upright. Do they? They can anticipate danger where we cannot, but can they anticipate death? Do they regret? What do they know? What do they feel? Physically, it is difficult to say since animals have astonishing reserves of strength, an ability to cope with injuries that would level an eighteen-wheeler. Rarely, do they even express pain, and then not for long. I know deer have consciousness, but what is that for them? They can't think the way I do. I don't have their consciousness, and they don't have mine. What is waiting to die like for an animal? What do they sense lying there? Do they experience being alone? White tail are not generally herd animals like elk and impala. Are they aware of familiar smells: the scent of an off-spring or mate, the gum smacking aroma of freshly planted roses, the scent of gun oil in the woods that heralds the start of hunting season? If it rains does the rain give comfort? If they land in the shade is there any relief? Is there any relief at all? Are they waiting to die, or do they just die?

*

I believe I was ten. Poppa took my hand and led me through the stand of ancient hemlocks as if I needed his protection. It was early spring. Daffodils had come up but lilacs were still a week away, mountain laurel three weeks from that. Jays were gone. Chickadees back. A blue heron fished the creek. We had to spray the dumpster with ammonia to keep a hungry bear at bay. Coyotes ambushed a raccoon near the chicken coop. All that was left of it were strands of grey and white hair. Coyotes eat everything but a gland in the anus. No sign of that, either. A morsel for something else.

Poppa normally never hesitated to talk about anything at all, but this morning he stayed silent as we walked, setting his feet as if he were hunting, almost reverent, unwilling to disturb the peace. We stopped at the edge of a clearing where Poppa indicated something out there with his chin. I couldn't see what he wanted me to see, but I followed him as he walked into the clearing until… There. Unclear to me until I moved closer. I had never seen anything like this before or since. Poppa had, but once. The bones of two massive deer, bucks with ten-point racks thick as cudgels, tangled, twisted, ultimately locked together, trapped, having fought until they died, socket to socket, smack against each other's sight and smell, socket to socket, until death. Much of the rest of them had been strewn about the clearing, vandalized by varmints, but those two skulls, now blind, remained, for eternity, locked in mortal combat.

I found this on an index card that fell on the kitchen floor near Mr. Coffee:

Talk to me of death

And I will tell you of a woodland dance

Hemlocks - a thick grove of them

A fitting place

A pas de deux - both dead

Like Romeo and Juliet

Only rivals

Beams eight points and ten

Thick as cudgels

Entangled by their horns

   And not their hearts

Titans locked in deadly battle

Crashing heads

Bucking for the "A" list

Eighteen tines tangled and trapped

Eye socket to eye socket

I called this place

> *Ozymandias*

Someone with that name

Ruled over ruins

This inscription left

> *On a piece of stone:*

"Look on my works and despair."

Seed unspread

Scattered bones

Picked clean

Antlers gnawed by mites

> *With yellow teeth*

Ozymandias

> *"Look on my works and despair"*

Scattered bones don't even get that.

The night before I left for Zimbabwe, we had a midnight snack of Hebrew National salami and Dr. Brown's cream soda in the breakfast nook. It was hard to leave home again, for both of us, but we never talked about it.

"T'ain't easy, MgGee," was all he'd say, a favorite quote from a favorite old radio show, Fibber MgGee and Molly. Digger O'Dell was also a character he loved. "It's Digger O'Dell, your friendly undertaker," Poppa crooned in an unctuous tone. "Nobody knows what evil lurks in the hearts of men, but the Shadow, he does." And then, *Muhahaha*. Poppa imitated the evil laugh perfectly.

We knew a family whose daughter had gone to South Africa to work for UNICEF. She was in an outlying village when she was stabbed to death.

"I'll be careful."

"Who said she wasn't careful?"

"Semper Fi," I said.

"Eat the apple, fuck the Corps."

"You don't mean that."

"I go back and forth. It gets confusing. When I was active duty, the Corps had a program where you learned to fly choppers with the rank of Warrant Officer. The curve ball was Viet-nam. You had to go there. It was just getting underway - most people didn't even know we were there - and I didn't have anything better to do nor did I yet have any opinions, so I gave it some thought. I knew a crew chief, gunny sergeant, old salt, hard core, who'd just come back and told him what I was thinking."

"'Don't,' he barked. Say what?"

"We landed the plane (Funny, how he referred to his chopper as a plane, but this was really early on, and that's what I remember), we landed the plane outside a friendly village to pick up a squad under fire. Our guys just made it, onloaded, and I gave the signal to lift off. But we couldn't, could not get off the ground because the villagers were hanging onto our runners. They wanted out. They knew the enemy would kill them or worse. We were taking fire. No choice. We turned the guns on them. Had to."

"Another time he shot an old woman in the head with his .45 as she tried to scramble aboard, "How'd I know she didn't have a bomb on her?""

"Thea, I never thought the person I'd kill would be an old lady, but I would have."

"Something else, if I'm gonna be absolutely truthful: too many rules, too many regulations. I've been a Marine all my life and expect to be for whatever's left of it. I still carry some of the principles the Corps taught me. I may be a demented old fool, but I am still ready, only thing is there's this serious problem, an attitude problem, my problem with authority. "You're an authority? Prove it!" This might be considered an impediment to success.

I never wanted to have to do something just because somebody else told me to do it. Not the best perspective under the circumstances."

Here's something. Poppa's a little kid. Five years old. He's on a school outing to the local police station where he proceeds to call the desk sergeant, "copper". His teacher tried to slap him but he ducked.

"Come on up here," said the sergeant, "I'm serious. Come on up here, or I'll lock you in the slammer and toss the key."

So, Poppa tells me, *I climb up there, and he sits me on his lap like my uncle. He smelled good, too - Old Spice - like my uncle.*

"Do you know why policemen like me are called coppers?" he asked me.

I didn't know what to say.

"No, sir," prodded my teacher.

I suppose I figured standing there like Denny Dimwit was preferable to doing what she wanted. I said nothing.

"The reason we're called coppers," explained the sergeant, "Is because long ago policemen wore jackets with copper buttons up and down the front. Look at this." The copper showed Poppa a picture of an old-timey policeman in his old-timey uniform and old-timey hat with a vertical row of copper buttons down the front of his tunic.

"You see?", he said, "Copper buttons. Coppers! Touch one."

Poppa did.

"Count them," he said, and counted with him: "one-two-three-four…"

Call a cop a name today, you'd get life if you're lucky.

So, Zimbabwe. A six-to-twelve-month assignment to head up a bush clinic where no villager had ever been vaccinated against anything. Food was bush meat and foraging. One can develop a taste for monkey. I second that. Fry 'em really really good. Flies supped on children's' eyes. Trichinosis crawled up through their feet. Lockjaw starved them. Vile water grumbled through their guts. Poppa once told me you could stand anything as long as you knew, at some point, it would be over. Zimbabwe was not a pleasant duty station, but it was gratifying, and I was bound to stay there.

That friend I talked about? The one I see often? Can you believe it? Believe it! I met him here. Here! In Zimbabwe. Deep in the bush. He was the closest doctor assigned to this place. It was not what I expected from Zimbabwe. He'd attended Howard as an undergrad then medical school at Yale. Very smart guy. He could have made millions on Park Avenue, but wanted to be where he was needed not where he was wanted. He was really funny, too, tended a ganja patch, and played a wicked guitar. What's not to like?

"Hey, Miss," Poppa wrote, "Wouldn't a nice, hot bath and a margarita be good right about now? I'm proud of ya, girl. If you ever get a day off, how 'bout we meet in Jo'burg for lunch? On me. I'm serious."

He meant it, too, but I was too far out in the bush to get anywhere at all aside from the local watering hole, and I mean "hole", as in where animals go to drink, not as in "bar", where men go to get stupid. When my first six months were up, I signed up for the second, but first…

"Hey, Miss, forget Jo'burg. How 'bout we meet in Florence? Italy! I'm serious. My bucket list. Pack up. What's the currency in Zimbabwe? Change to lira. Ticket waiting at the airport." He always wanted to go there, Florence, I think mostly because Sophie Rose, my grandmother, could have been Botticelli's inspiration for Venus borne by the sea, her pale skin and red hair showed her to have arrived from a world that wasn't ours. Poppa always got a look of beatitude when he spoke of her this way. She was as graceful as seagrass underwater. She always looked to Poppa the way she looked when he first saw her sitting by her lonesome as he carried his burger and fries past her table. She was his "Song of Songs".

Of all the sights in Florence, Michelangelo's David cast a spell over the man. It stood by itself in a rotunda known as the Academia, at the end of a hall lined with the heavily muscled bodies of sculpted slaves emerging from massive rocks. Some think these are as powerful as the David himself, but Poppa wasn't one of them. He stood there daily studying David's face, eyes focused on the giant in the distance, sling over his shoulder. What was he thinking? Was he plotting the trajectory of his missile? Heavy enough to kill. Light enough to fly. Rotations needed to meet the distance. Angle of descent. Angle of release. The head's the target. He's wearing a helmet. The kill spot's a small one. Breathe. Focus. Calm. When Poppa did David's inner monologue for me I thought back to when the sniper in my outfit told me that if I heard his shot he wasn't aiming at me. Would that have been David's position?

True to form, Poppa managed to embarrass himself or would have embarrassed himself had he been "embarrassable". We'd been in Italy a week when Poppa decided his command of the language was prescient, perhaps akin to savant. He jumped right in, his accent a showstopper. Commendable? I guess, but risky. So what? How else do you learn? His words.

Calzone was the specialty of a small trattoria and bar in Fiesole, a hill village north of Florence. Calzone. Spiced, fresh pizza dough folded over melted ricotta or mozzarella and prosciutto or sausage and peppers or anything else you want short of a Hebrew National hot dog. Poppa said let's give it a try. We took the bus from the Duomo. Half hour, tops. The bus let us off practically in front of the trattoria where the famous calzone awaited. Poppa led the way. Once through the door, he spread his arms wide and announced in a voice you could hear over a bank of kettle drums, "Voglio un grande cazzone!" The place shut down in shock. Mouths froze open, food half chewed, beer bottles mid-way... Not one single syllable. Not one sound. Poppa bellowed again, "Voglio un grande cazzone!", proudly certain he was ordering a large calzone. He was not. He was asking for a grande cazzone - CAZZONE - a Big Cock. C-O-C-K. "Voglio un grande cazzone!" I want a big cock! Twice. The place went berserk. Poppa was a star. Instead of arresting him as a public nuisance, wine and calzones were on the house. Everybody got tiddly. Poppa prided himself on having expanded Italian American relations. We left the place two very happy tourists shitfaced and stuffed.

*

From a hotel in Florence, Italy on sheets with an astronomical thread count to a hammock in a mud hut in Zimbabwe - the story of my life. The story of Poppa's life, too. My middle name should have been Reuben Henry. Another quote Poppa passed on: "Life is a banquet, and most poor sons of bitches are starving to death." It was his creed, and so it became my creed, too. So little time in which to do it all! I had to leave home to get started.

I am the blood of Reuben Henry. We wrote to each other often about the big stuff, and Aunt Gert kept me posted on the small.

Chapter 12

HOME

"Here's your beer. Here's your smokes. Pork rinds. Tums. Where's he at?"

"Packin'," answered Gertie.

"What do you mean, 'packing'"?

"Packing. As in folding clothes and stuffing them into something called a suitcase, or a duffle bag, or an old kit bag, depending on what era you're currently in."

"Are you trying to tell me something?"

"He's been quiet lately. Seems lost sometimes. Not like north, south, east, and west lost, but more like in some other world."

*

"What's up, Poppa," I asked, giving him a hug. He hugged me back, strong as ever.

"I assume you left the world a better place."

"Left 'em dancing in the streets. You going somewhere?"

"West By God Virginia. Ever heard of it?"

"Gimme a break, old man."

"Smile when you say that," he said in his trademark gangster impersonation.

"You're going to West Virginia?"

"Nope. We're going to West Virginia, land of our forebears."

"How do you know I don't have anything else to do?"

"You're between assignments."

"Your point is?"

"We'll take the truck and alternate driving."

He did a little jig to the words of Steely Dan, "Drink scotch whiskey all night long and die behind the wheel…"

"That's not in my plans," I said.

You're gonna love West Virginia, Toots. Besides, the old man needs this. There's ghosts down there. Good ones. Only good ones. Not to worry. Haven't seen them forever. Time you all got to know each other."

"You're kidding.

"Right. I'm kidding. You got me."

West Virginia

Poppa sat in the suicide seat, and I drove. It was a major pick-up - a Ford 350 - hard on fuel, hard on turns, but monster bad and comfortable. We were on our way to West By God.

I drove the most tedious stretch of the way through the mountains of western Pennsylvania. An eternity of concrete. Poppa took over when we turned south through Wheeling and followed the Monongahela River to Morgantown where he'd graduated WVU better than half a century ago. More. Back then it was a small, main street, old time mountain town, nothing pretty about it but sturdy enough. Now, no more mom 'n' pops or even Main Street, for that matter, but a macadam speedway called Monongahela Boulevard with a McDonald's at one end and Arby's at the other. R. B. Roast. Beef. RB. RB's. Arby's. Get it? How many ways can you say, 'roast beef'?

"They got Costco now," he remarked sardonically and with more than a tinge of regret, although, another thing about Poppa - he didn't regret much. Let's put it this way: he did not chew his regrets over and over like cud. He acknowledged, made amends, moved on, and tried never to do it again, except, being human, he couldn't escape doing it again. But it was not for trying. The man did his best.

We didn't go through Charleston because he didn't see the point. We were headed somewhere else. Where the magic tree is. Was. Why dawdle?

"I ever tell you about Crockett?" he wanted to know.

"No."

"Probably did."

"Tell me again."

"You're too young."

"For what?"

"Your memory's on the way out."

"What'd you say your name was, old man?"

"Funny."

*

Crockett. Crockett E. Lee. His father named him after Davy. His mother was somehow related to the confederate general, but, since they were dirt poor and white, that didn't seem likely. Had they been Black? Maybe. Lookit Thomas Jefferson. Who Crockett really looked like was that kid on the Andy Griffith show who grew up to be a famous movie director - goofy grin, freckles, a lick of hair. Handy with a fishing pole. Could spit through his teeth. Didn't chew tobacco but looked like he tried it.

Poppa spent his boyhood in the hills around North Fork. How many hours had he and Crockett clocked out there in the woods armed with home-made slingshots taking target practice on squirrels and that flock of crows that was always around? Crockett had a way of making a slingshot out of a single wire hanger and a slice of inner tube. Once that hangar was twisted into shape, it could launch a stone like a bullet. Ball bearings, if Crockett could get his hands on some, were deadly. The boys would show up, crows would squall and scatter, only to return when the boys fooled them by sitting still. They were best friends, shared cheese sandwiches and butter crunch bars, and swore to be faithful.

For a while there it was *Crockett Crockett Crockett*. Crockett could make the planet's best slingshot. Crockett found a secret fishing hole. Crockett could play the spoons. Crockett's uncle was a professional wrestler in Scranton. Crockett's mother won a bake prize at the fair for her strawberry-rhubarb pie. Crockett Crockett Crockett. Crockett came and went with nobody but Reuben Henry being the only person in the family to have ever seen him. One night he was invited for dinner. The house fried chicken special, Crockett's favorite - fried chicken - only Crockett never showed up. "He was coming down with a cold and maybe fell asleep," offered Reuben Henry.

Reuben Henry and Crockett had this secret. The two of them. Nobody else had a single solitary clue - their own tree, a honey locust hidden deep within a grove of Virgin Hemlocks way back in the Tug River Forest. On the day of a full moon when its leaves were golden, Reuben Henry and Crockett would make their way to the secret tree and, with a secret key from a dead conquistadores' chest, unlock a secret door in the trunk of the honey locust, and retrieve a secret wooden horse. They'd spend the rest of the day 'til dinner hammering precious jewels onto the horse - rubies, emeralds, sapphires, pearls, and diamonds. They named their steed, Bucephalus, the name Alexander the Great gave his war horse. Come dinner, they'd put Bucephalus back in the tree, lock it tight, add slabs of bark as camouflage, and go home to eat. The two boys grew apart, and Poppa said he hadn't been there ever since.

So much of him had been formed there, his hard scrabble side, his ability to know a lie when he heard one, his unwillingness to suffer ignorance and hypocrisy. West Virginians had a lot of crap in their systems, no doubt about it, but they knew what true labor was, had no tolerance for slackers, and certainly did not suffer fools gladly. Poppa believed keep your mouth shut or suffer the consequences.

"You think Crockett might still be around?" I asked, "Maybe look him up. Why not?"

"Why not?"

"Sure, Why not?"

"Why not is if he's not dead he's close to it. Tell you what: let's find that tree."

After a while he said, "Actually, there's somebody else I'd like to see."

"Who is he?"

"Her," he answered.

Cinder Bottom

They didn't really live in Cinder Bottom, the Negro part of town, just kept a crib there. Mostly they lived with us. Her name was Hazel Franklin, and Miz Franklin had a daughter my age named Sweet, Sweet Franklin, just that. Sounds like incense. Frankincense. "The perfumed tincture of the roses." Her mother worked for my grandmother in the boarding house. The Supreme Court had ordered integration of the school system, so, since there wasn't but one school in the whole place, anyway, Sweet and I wound up in the same class, so we were around each other quite a bit. She'd even help out some, with the cooking or the sheets and towels boiling out back. We were easy around each other, sweet and sour, kind of like siblings, except the time came when Sweet filled out her two dresses so Miz Franklin never kept her busy eyes off us could she help it. If Sweet and I were alone in a room together, Miz Franklin charged through like a water buffalo. I didn't know what the fuss was all about until suddenly I did.

Sweet was really beautiful. I never thought of it before but she was. Sweet was beautiful. We were both tall, about the same height. She had high cheekbones, a long neck, the posture of a ballerina, and a body made for high hurdles at which she was county champ. A gold medalist became her mentor. She would have gone to the Olympics had she not met me. We were always together, so it was obvious we were friends, although there was nothing physical about it. We'd never yet touched each other. Terror ruled, not the Klan type terror but the terror of wondering what we'd gotten ourselves into.

We never said what we felt. She would be my first, and I hers. It seemed so sweet and pure. Being around each other was all we needed. We were naive. Some people did not like what they saw. Eventually, that took its toll. There was so much we couldn't do together. Even so.

School officials had approved the attendance of its graduating seniors at a political science consortium in Washington, D.C. Sweet and I were graduating seniors, ergo, there we were, away from home, in a city that didn't care if we held hands while waiting in line to tour the White House. Our first night at the hotel we said good night and wished we hadn't. The second night I sneaked into her room. The third night she sneaked into mine. We knew it was dangerous, yet that gave it no edge. It was frightening the way a dream is frightening when you can't wake up and you know it's real but it's not. We didn't choose to be in love with each other. We didn't plan on it. We didn't even want it. It was gut level, so dear, so delicate, so right, so achingly real.

Once we got back, the guys started treating me weird, like I knew something that they wanted to know, and they'd promise to be my best friend if I'd tell them. Finally, one of them came out with it,

"You dicked that bitch, didn't you, Ace? How 'bout some 'tang for your main man here?"

My arm cut loose like a catapult. I hit that goddamn peckerwood so hard, broke his goddamn jaw. Heard it crack. If you're a Jew amongst the Philistines, young lady, best be quick. I got suspended from school for that one, even though it wasn't on school property. Nothing fair about it. The other guy said I started it, and they believed him. They sent me home for a week which was fine with me. It was like parole. I had to follow the rules, or else they'd send me back. However, since I had to go back, anyway, I had no compunction about breaking any if the occasion presented.

Sweet was really weird about it. I asked her if she wanted to do homework, but she said she'd already done it.

"Want to see if we can beat the guy on Jeopardy?"

"Uh, uh."

"What's wrong?"

Sweet just looked at me and shook her head.

One day she was late coming home. It got dark, and she still wasn't home. Not like her. We began to get worried and fanned out to search for her - flashlights, lanterns, bullhorns. The police joined in with dogs and found her stuffed into a culvert, still alive but badly disfigured from the knife slashes that scarred her cheeks. An ear and her nose had been cut off. When Sweet's mother saw her, she collapsed and screamed with anguish. *How could they do this? How could they do this? My baby! My baby!* I can still hear that scream. I hear it like it was right now, like being obliterated by a freight train.

Sweet would recover, but she'd have to live this way for the rest of her life. I didn't care. I just wanted her to live. She wouldn't let me see her. She wouldn't let anybody see her. Late one night, between shifts, Sweet sneaked from her hospital bed. She took a sheet with her. They found her in the stairwell hanging by that sheet. She tied it around a rail, jumped, and broke her neck. Whoever ambushed her got away with it. Didn't matter people knew who it was.

"Sorry about your girlfriend," they said.

I think she knew something would happen, just not what did. Her mother wouldn't talk to me, wouldn't look at me. Her funeral was closed casket. When I approached her coffin with a bouquet of white roses, Miz Franklin tore them from my hand and pushed me away, told me *get the hell out*. She never showed up at the boarding house again, never came back, disappeared someplace else.

I never went back to that school. I knew I'd kill somebody. I'd hear something. I'd know something. No. It was better to put serious distance between me and them. I enlisted and got my GED on The Rock, which was what we called the island of Okinawa, one dismal duty station, but as far away as I could get. A three-year hitch was better than a life sentence. Always have had a good head for figures.

But God damn the people who would do such a thing, who could do such a thing! I was walking across campus one day - this was after my discharge - when I spotted a girl who looked like she might've been a girl who would do this. She was across the quad. What was her name? Didn't we have Mr. Ditman for geometry? Somebody told me she had a crush on me. Classes were changing, so the walkways were congested. Couldn't get through and lost track of her. I thought I was nuts and wrote it off. Until I saw her again. It wasn't Mr. Ditman's geometry class. It was the girls' varsity basketball team. She was tall, like Sweet, and, like Sweet, she was on the team. I began to follow her around. I didn't know why but I couldn't help myself. After a couple of weeks, I knew her every move, but I still did not know why. One afternoon I waited outside a coffee shop while she was inside. Why was I even there? What did I intend to do? Nothing. I didn't intend to do a thing. She walked out of the shop and looked directly at me, then crossed the street to where I was standing and got right up in my face.

"Why the fuck are you following me?"

"I watched you play ball. North Fork Public High. Sweet Franklin was your teammate."

"That's you?"

"Good call."

"Too bad, huh? Sweet Franklin, right?"

"I thought you might like to reminisce about our days at dear old Tug High."

"Meaning what?"

"Meaning, who killed her?"

The blood drained from her face as if a floor had collapsed beneath her.

"She killed herself," she said then pulled a little twenty-two auto on me, a corn popper, yeah, but aimed right... "Case closed. Stay the the fuck out of my face, or, so help me God…" She could well have pulled the trigger, she was that shook.

"It was a terrible thing. I thought you might have a flashback, some contemplation, a past memory, something like that."

She thought I was crazy. I was.

"Don't blink, schmuck. I'm going to back away. If you ever come near me again, it's self-defense."

"Practice makes perfect," Poppa said as she turned and walked away.

*

"How do you know she did it?" I asked Poppa.

"They *all* did it," was his answer.

Chapter 13

Poppa's Grove

"If I'd been born a thousand years ago I'd've been a Druid. As a kid what we did was we climbed trees, me 'n' Crockett, every tree we could we climbed. Set up high on a branch and dangle our legs. White tail walked below without suspecting we were there. A cub came by, too. Black bear. Smaller than a cocker spaniel. Where was its mom we didn't know but we did know not to climb down until it'd been gone a good half hour. Couple times we sneaked a beer, chugged it, belched, had a belching contest, and laughed so hard, lucky we stayed put and didn't fall.

"When your grandma and I moved here full time I planted an oak to celebrate. Look at it now, that's one mighty big tree. Got history. An oak leaf cluster is a military rank. I love this tree. I love them all but something about an oak says eternity to me. It keeps its leaves late in the season, later than the young maples, later than the dogwood, later than the apple trees, Macoun and honey crisp, the red ones not the green. They stay longer. Oak turns a deep reddish-copper color and holds that color way before they fall. Squirrels hide the acorns. Planted it when it was the size of a pencil. That little hollow at the base of the trunk? That's where you'll put my ashes, right there."

The oak was at one end of Poppa's special grove of trees, ones he'd planted to celebrate life's events noteworthy and marvelous. Every miracle - birth, death, and the ones in between - occasioned a new tree. He'd pick and shovel the perfect hole, mix a soil of his own concoction specifically for this particular tree, laid in three or four dead trout for fertilizer: a pear for their anniversary, a cherry tree for Sophie Rose's birthday, a weeping peasblossom for my mother, Katherine Rose, when she was born, a peach tree when I was born, a Japanese maple with its dark wine nearly black leaves also for my mother, this one in her memory. He cross- bred a wild blueberry patch at the south end between two stout white birch. Poppa hauled blue stone and shale down the mountain and up from the creek and fashioned a bench to rest in the middle.

"I ever tell you about my pet squirrel?" he asked me one day.

"Tell me."

"You ain't gonna believe it."

"Try me."

"I was maybe eleven, twelve, maybe. I had this particular oak tree that felt right, which is where I went to be by myself. Even Crockett didn't know, but he could've found me had he wanted but he knew not to. Anyway, I was eleven or twelve…"

"You said that."

"Do you mind?"

"Go ahead."

"I'm sitting under this oak. It was summer, late summer, but, still, a little chilly. If you know to be still you will see wonderful things. Once, I swear, this itty-bitty fawn comes wandering by, picking its way, heading in my direction. Right at me. Right at me! I am stone. Didn't move. Didn't breathe. Kept my eyes straight ahead, right on him as, I swear to God, this little thing comes right up on me, face to face, nose to nose. Just remember these things can hear you from a quarter mile away and smell you from even further, yet here was this itty-bitty baby white tail about on top of me. I thought about touching him, but the wind shifted and helped him figure out what I was. Flash. Bang. Gone. Disappeared like a mote of dust."

"Didn't I hear you say something about a squirrel?"

"Sweetheart, this is not "cut to the chase" like on TV. Process not product."

"Squirrels?"

"Ever eat one?"

"Do I want to?"

"They hunted them in West Virginia, Kentucky, Tennessee... Cook 'em like fried chicken only with mashed sweets and greens instead of whites and beans. Go for the head with a .22. Not much of a target, like shooting at a silver dollar. Had to be a dead-on shot. Didn't want to mess up any meat because there wasn't that much to begin with. We're talking ten, fifteen yards. You try it."

"I ate peanut butter rice with pangolin and ghee. You try it."

"What's pangolin?"

"I didn't know then, and I don't want to know now. Anyway, we were talking squirrels."

"Fine. I'm sitting on the south side of the trunk because wild turkeys were roosting on the north. The ground below their roost was covered with turkey pucky, so I sure as hell wasn't about to sit in it."

"Squirrels?"

"You're getting bossy."

"Can't help myself. You got me hooked."

"A whole pack of squirrels was scurrying on a tree opposite where I was. Well, no lie, one of those nutcrackers stops mid trunk, stares at me, and begins to chatter. So, I chatter back. I'm so good at it, he chatters. I chatter. He chatters. I chatter. He doesn't. He's being truly cautious, inching down the trunk, hesitating before each step, stops on a ground root, stares at me, and chatters. I give it my best chatter back. We're maybe ten feet apart. He chatters. I chatter. We've got us a duet. Puccini. Mozart. Groucho and

Harpo. The Two Stooges. Next thing he's hopping towards me, clambers up my shoulder, and, no lie, takes a seat. Takes a seat! Just sits there. I don't know for how long, although what he did up there I also don't know but I doubt it was anything special, and I don't know why he stopped doing it. He didn't say a word, just climbed back down, and skipped on over and up his tree."

"You've got a way with animals, Mr. Reuben Henry."

"We got a way with each other, young lady."

The Time He Embarrassed the Living Shit Out of Me

Or would have. I'm twelve years old heading into junior high. I come home one day after school and Poppa's really excited, cannot wait to tell me what he was dying to tell me.

"We're in luck, Thea. You're never gonna guess why, so I'm gonna tell you, that is, unless you'd like to guess."

"You're building a still in the back."

"Close but no cigar. Ready?"

I Steeled Myself.

"I bought a hot dog cart and got a license to sell hot dogs from the parking lot at your new school. I'm calling it, *Mr. Hot Dog Man.* Got a banner in your school's colors. *Mr. Hot Dog Man.* Dig it? Great, huh?"

Great? I thought I would die. No. No. I take that back. I *knew* I would die. How could he do this to me? You think the kids at school would ever let me forget this? Gramps sells hot dogs from a cart in the parking lot? Please, let me die.

"So, what do you think?", he asked.

I think I want to die. I <u>know</u> I want to die."

"I don't get it."

"Mr. Hot Dog Man?"

"Catchy, huh?"

Something suddenly clicked. I said, "You're kidding, right?"

"You don't like the idea?"

"Tell me you're kidding."

"Why would I lie to you?"

"You wouldn't."

"Right."

"So?"

"Gotcha goin' there, didn't I, Toots?"

"You and I would part company. Don't do this to me ever again."

"Do what?"

"Do what? You will go down in flames."

"'Top of the world, Ma. Top of the world.' James Cagney. *White Heat.*"

"Thank you."

"Welcome."

*

I wanted to know if Poppa believed in God. Not that I did, exactly, but it had been on my mind. We were always sitting and talking at that breakfast nook one way or the other.

"God?", he winced.

"You know who I mean."

"*What,* you mean."

"Thank you for the clarification."

"Do I believe in God?", he repeated my question. "Well, once I did."

"Once?"

"Sort of."

"You first," I said.

"It was in Alaska. Way up the Yukon. Middle of nowhere. Back then my favorite place to be. Peace on earth. Good will to men, as long as they stayed a long way away. I'd been in touch with a guy from Hollywood who wanted one of my stories. We spoke before I left.

"I'll be able to reach you, right?" he asked.

Of course, I had to tell him *no way*.

"Meaning what?"

"Meaning no way in Athapaskan."

Man was absolutely flummoxed that, in the late twentieth century, with all the gear at Radio Shack, he would not be able to reach me.

"I get it," he said. "I can't call you, but you'll be able to call me, right? Got to be a pay phone somewhere up there, right?"

"You're never gonna win on Jeopardy," was my answer.

"You'll read the trades, right?"

I shrugged.

"You mean you're not even going to read the trades?" he asked, absolutely dumbfounded. Talk about a jaw drop! That actor who played the ghost of Jacob Marley in *A Christmas Carol?* He had to tie up his jaw to keep it from falling open.

"See you in a month," I said. "Or so."

So, here I am a day away from any other human being. I'd been walking pretty much since daybreak, and now it was nearly dark. I was tired and hungry enough to drop down on the spot and settle in for the night. Tea with sugar, beef jerky, dried apricots, a Baby Ruth. I spread out a caribou skin I'd packed in, my sleeping bag on top of that, took off my boots, crawled inside, and zipped up, although not before torching a doobie given me by a young Athapaskan woman who thought I was Al Pacino, and who I could have taken advantage of but did not. I fired up, lay back, and fixed on a sky filled with bobbing and weaving northern lights, the aurora borealis, great curtains of light dancing with abandon. Keep your Ambien, folks. I fell asleep that way."

"Nice."

"Penthouse on Park? Condo in the Keys? Beachfront Riviera? Gimme a caribou skin and a fat doobie."

"I thought we were talking about God?"

"Weren't we?"

NORTH FORK

North Fork was never much of anywhere, and it still wasn't. The boarding house had long since come down. In its place was a trucking business featuring roll on-roll off containers. Hermanson Street was still there but was now nothing but an open lot with the promise that a new Thrifty Six Motel would rise in its place any day now.

"It's like seeing ghosts on every corner. I can see them but they can't see me," he said as we cruised from street to street. "It's all here but nothing's left."

"Do you think your tree's still there, the one you had with Crockett? Do you think Crockett's even there?" I asked.

"He ain't if he's smart," replied Poppa, "Of course, Crockett was never too bright. His IQ went down in the winter when the temperature dropped. Hot dog with a slingshot, that's for sure. We both had keys, but I think he lost his."

"Where is that tree, anyway, Poppa?"

"Gotta find it," he said. "Pedal to the medal, darlin'."

"I don't want a ticket."

"Needn't worry about that one, Kiddo," he chortled. "Cops here can't hardly write a single word. Tell the truth, I don't believe they can even spell *God*.

There was this girl - what was known as a *Back Porch Baptist*. We became friends after I reassured her that neither I nor any other Jew was a rapist with horns. I swear, though, she could not stop looking. She was all, 'Jesus was against this and this and Jesus was for this and this. Pat Robertson was chosen by the Lord to be the fount of righteous bigotry for too many *pious* people, like her, and I liked her, not romantic like but she was lively and a good person, and I never heard her talk trash about anyone. Could not, would not have stood it if she did. One day - we were talking salvation - she was crying because I was doomed - I asked her about the *Sermon On The Mount*. She looked at me dumbfounded.

What's that?" she asked.

What's that? The Sermon On The Mount? What's that? Gobsmacked!!!

"His very words," I told her. "Blessed are the merciful for they shall obtain mercy. Salt of the earth. Whosoever is angry with his brother without cause. Love thy neighbor. Turn the other cheek - that one."

"Which one?"

"You never heard of it? Your main man in the pulpit never preached it?"

"He preaches prosperity and the wages of sin."

"But not the *Sermon On The Mount*. Damn, girl, I'm Jewish, and I've read the whole thing twice."

"Then, you're a better Christian than I am," she said.

"God, forbid," I muttered.

*

We'd seen enough of North Fork. After a stop for liver sandwiches at Yokum's Beanery, we took a back road (as if there were any other kind) out of town to the Tug River Forest. Poppa began singing, "In the Blue Ridge Mountains of Virginia, stood a cow on a railroad track..." He pictured an old-fashioned steam locomotive with a cow catcher. Appalachian Spring. I actually smelled things growing, aromas familiar and unknown, sometimes tart, sometimes sweet. Wild daisies, Queen Anne's Lace, milkweed, fiddleheads, and ferns.

"You didn't know, did you, that Queen Anne's Lace was the original carrot? Next time you see one pluck it out by the roots that are kind of fungal like, big as a jellybean, and dirty white. Scratch the roots with your fingernail then smell it. Just like a carrot, right? Try it. It's not thick or crisp, or long and orange, nor might you welcome it anywhere near your salad but it is a carrot. Cherokee knew how good they were. Out of mud, such beauty. Park here," he said.

I pulled off the road into a clearing.

"Why here?" I asked.

"Know some place better?" he answered, pushed open the door with his shoulder, jumped down from the truck spry as a grunt (or wished he was), and took off straight into the woods.

"Wait up," I shouted.

"The lazy bird gets no worm," he called back but never stopped.

"Do you know where you're going?" I caught up to him and asked.

"Does any of us know where we are going?" he answered.

"That's bullshit. Not worthy of you."

"We still gotta find that tree," he said.

"Only four hundred square miles to go," I said.

"Oh, ye of little faith."

"Faith takes truth."

"Then it's not faith," he said, took out a compass, and turned west.

"Where are we going?"

"West."

"Why west?"

"Ours is not to question why, ours is just to do or die."

"You're as full of shit as a Christmas turkey," I said.

"Nice. You used to think I knew what I was talking about," he said.

"How old was I then? Seven? Eight? Nine?"

"Watch your mouth."

"I learned from the master."

"Suppose I've been wrong? All this time. Wrong. Just suppose? I wonder," he said.

I didn't answer, and he didn't pursue it. He stopped where he was and bent over to look at something.

"See this mushroom here?" he explained. "See that tree over there? They're in cahoots with each other. I'll scratch your back. You scratch mine. Go along to get along."

We were losing light when somewhere out there a terrible screech sliced the silence.

"Owl and rabbit," Poppa said, "Tooth 'n' nail. Law of the jungle."

"We're Losing light."

He took a flashlight from his pocket.

"Start looking for specks of light head high on the trees. Me 'n' Crockett bought these glow-in-the-dark thumb tacks at the five and dime so we could find it in the dark. Look sharp."

"You're the one who best look sharp. I don't know where in the hell we are."

A chill had begun to set in. I don't think we had but an hour of light left. I didn't mind the chill. I didn't even mind if we spent the night in the woods. Done it before. I was wearing lined jeans, good socks, a USMC beanie, and a down vest, so I wasn't worried, plus a super-sized bag of MnM's in my pocket clambering for freedom. I didn't want to think what I was thinking but thoughts come in on you like the motion of the ocean. You can't stop them. I began to wonder if this were Poppa's imagination - Crockett, the tree, Bucephalus. What else? The instant this thought came to me, the pit of my stomach dove into freefall. Once, when I realized I was a nanosecond away from a head-on collision on the freeway, I felt a gut-wrenching fear - panic - such as I'd never felt before or since until that moment in the woods when I knew Poppa was a human being of indeterminate grace, nonetheless, encroaching on his infirmities at a steady crawl.

Where was this Goddamn tree? This sacred honey locust husbanding a magic horse. Should I have been coddling his delusion? I didn't even know if it was a delusion. What I knew was that I was following a beam of light deeper and deeper into a dark wood.

He began to sing, *"Davy, Davy Crockett, king of the wild frontier…"* and soon shined his light on a tree that revealed a button of bright light just about as high as a human head. Then another. We were following a path of every third tree. The canopy covered the stars, but tiny dots of light traced our way. A little child shall lead them. That's what Poppa was now. I followed him and lost my fear. I could hear the creek rushing some distance in front of us. Even though dusk was imminent, the creek reflected the remaining light so that this portion of the earth gently glowed. I could see the willow trees on opposite banks of the creek a few yards ahead of us. The trees met overhead, so their branches hung down together and fell loosely to the ground like a closely beaded curtain hanging in a wide doorway. These were trees that might once have been worshiped, dense and thick, trunks wide around as tractor tires, twisted in parts like hawser ropes, blistered with boles like plump, gray warts. Walking through those hanging branches was like passing through the veil.

"We went to the other side," said Poppa. Then he stuck his flashlight under his chin to create a monster face and did a Boris Karloff.

"Want to join me?" he croaked.

I gawked at him.

"You must think I'm crazy," said Poppa.

"Prove me wrong."

"Break out those M&M's first."

By this time in my life, I'd had a trunk full of dubious experiences and coped with all of them, not always well, but still. Yet, to me, that night, nearly night, it was spooky as hell following the old man through that willow green curtain, really layers and layers of curtains, with no sense of a center, like moving through fields of wheat and corn that are completely over your head. How was I supposed to know where I was?

"We're going in circles," I said.

"Smaller and smaller."

"On purpose?"

"Shh."

"I'm still waiting for you to prove me wrong," I told him.

We stepped into a clearing with an opening in the canopy that allowed a shaft of filtered light, as if a magician had snapped his fingers and said, "Shazaam, let there!" In the middle of the clearing was the honey locust tree, and that shaft of sunlight made that honey locust glow. It was wondrous.

"I wish Crockett could see this," said Poppa, "Come look."

He took my hand and showed me a wrought iron door knocker attached to the trunk to alert the wooden horse when they were outside.

"I can't remember how to get in there anymore," he said. Rueful. Wistful.

"Do you want to?"

"It was a pretty thing."

"Is this the place?"

"What place?"

"That perfect peace place."

"No. It's a place. One place. I loved the way those jewels glittered, sun or no sun. I loved it. I loved Crockett, and Crockett loved me. Here's a newsflash, Toots. Advice from a really smart old friend. Fascinating woman. One of the first female war correspondents in Europe during World War Two. She knew what she was talking about. Don't throw up when you hear it. Promise?"

"Promise."

"Cross your heart?"

"Speak!"

You must maintain some image of magnificence in your heart.

"It took a while," he said, "But I finally figured out peace is portable. Recharge the batteries daily and keep it with you, and not like that ridiculous electric bunny. I'm serious. The prize is the surprise."

"What's the prize?"

"It's a surprise."

Chapter 14

NEW YORK CITY

I needed a break and took one. My friend? The guy from Zimbabwe? That Doctors Without Borders guy? I begged off on a post to Mongolia, decided on a little New York City R & R instead, and managed to see seven Broadway shows in six days with him which would have paid for a month's scuba diving in Belize, not that I wanted to go to Belize, anyway, or anyplace like it since the bulk of my life has been spent getting accustomed to monkey meat.

Here's something else about Zimbabwe - bush wine, a village tradition. Only a certain family was allowed to brew it subject to a secret recipe passed down for generations. The fruit they plucked and squashed was then mixed with *"eye of newt" and "toe of frog"* and random vegetation on the cusp of rot. Drink enough of it, and you will do anything. We - my friend and I - might have had a little fling in the bushes, but I can't remember, or don't want to, and he hasn't said anything about it, either.

Mongolia, Chad, any of the *stans* would have kept me out of the USA and therefore too much out of touch for way too long. The Big Apple was the way to go. I even wore a dress, considered heels but decided on a stylish court shoe instead, and I got to wear perfume instead of mosquito repellent. A touch here. A touch there. Mosquito repellent, you've got to take a bath in it. Back in Zimbabwe, they'd circle overhead like drones while they decided to eat you on the spot or carry you back to their nest.

We had a pretty good time, I must say, this friend of mine and myself. Some badly needed R & R with a member of the same outfit. How come? It was, simply, the best idea at the time. I don't know what else it was. I needed a break. Love at first sight? Nope. Maybe third or fourth sight? Maybe, but who needs to think about it? A luxury hotel! Better. Clean sheets. Even better. Jacuzzi. Oh, boy. Room service. Champagne and brie? Some place that wasn't made of wattle and cattle dung. One of the plays we saw was written by an old girlfriend of his. The male lead came out dressed in Levi's, a corduroy sports jacket, blue work shirt, and desert boots. Uncanny. This guy sitting next to me was wearing the exact same thing! He wanted us to go backstage afterwards. We did. She smiled graciously. Interesting face, but I really don't know what he saw in her. Jealous? Not really. My life hadn't always been so reasonable, either.

The best theater we saw starred an actress friend of my friend's and her husband, *Happy Days,* by Sam Beckett. Strange play. Strange playwright. But, compelling. If there's a production of anything of his anywhere near where I happen to be, I'll buy the ticket. Can't do that in Mongolia or Zimbabwe. No show biz. That's their downside. I can even see a place in the multi-verse for Doris Day. And I did once see a production of *King Lear* in Finland. Best I've seen. A real pleasure to be in that audience. Many years later I took myself to see Glenda Jackson's *Lear* for my birthday. To quote Big Daddy from *Cat on A Hot Tin Roof,* "Mendacity!" Or, as Floyd and

Lloyd would say, "Bullshit. Ain't nothin' but chewed up grass." Given Shakespeare's language, why would an actor play a mute and *speak* with his fingers? Jesus. Another great one was *Three Sisters* in Hungary. I'd never seen anything like it. Still haven't. At key dramatic moments, a gong would strike, the actors would freeze, and dried leaves would fall to the stage, at first, only one, but at each interval more and more, until, at the very end, the stage was filled with them as the three sisters joined hands and skipped with a hint of desperation in a circle through the pile of leaves, still enamored with the illusion of moving to Moscow. To this day the irony of their situation evokes the pain I felt then. Another thing New York City has over Zimbabwe are restaurants - Jewish, Polish, Russian, Thai, Chinese, Ethiopian, thick steaks, rare fish, vegetables never imagined - succulence du jour. I especially like the ones where they don't say, "Hi. I'll be your server…" I already know who you are. Just deliver my dish hot and soon. It's fun, sure, as long as I don't think about what they have to eat in places where I work. Monkey meat, filet of hippo, bush pig…Save me some! Just kidding. Truth is - I've said it before - as much fun as celebrity restaurants can be, I'm just as happy at a diner - booth no stool - grilled cheese, fries, and a cherry coke. Maybe apple pie. Poppa told me back in the 80's he refused to eat in any joint that served creme brulee. No wonder I am the way I am. I had Key Lime Pie at the bar where Hemingway hung out. Big disappointment. Hemingway, too. *"Wouldn't it be pretty to think so?"* What's that? I still don't get it. *Death in the Afternoon* was a good one. Actually, I'm a Bronte' fan. These days, from my perspective, Heathcliffe was a narcissistic little prick.

*

One evening, at dinner, his dimples seemed to dance off the wine glass and wink at me.

*

New York is a city for walking, so we walked everywhere. Its charm was on the way out as prices were on the way up, as bodegas gave way to Whole Foods, known to some as Whole Paycheck, and Tower Records sank. The apartment my grandparents had on Morton Street for $750/month was now at $3,000. Bleecker Street had been replaced by antiseptic high rises with gyms and pools and workstations, $7,200 per month. Are they nuts? Christopher Street used to be a lot of fun but now it was all retail. The Cubby Hole was still on the corner of Morton and Hudson, a lesbian bar that opened while Poppa and my grandmother Sophie Rose first lived there. Poppa told a story about how my grandmother always laughed when she told the story of coming home one night when she was approached by a dumpy, Dickie's attired woman who sidled up to her asking, "Where's the Hubby Club?".

Chapter 15

Back Home

Aunt Gert called.

"He shot Dub Tuttle."

"Killed Him?"

"Birdshot. Got him in the ass, It'll sting for a while. Doc's currently picking it out with tick tweezers."

"Where's Poppa now?"

"Hospital."

"He got hurt?"

"No. He's fine. Physically. Trooper Colby convinced the powers that be that Poppa should be in the hospital and not in jail, so he's resting comfortably at Hudson-Greene, sixth floor, psych. Colby's still with him. Rent a car and get up here, chop chop."

I drove straight to the hospital.

"Where's my bucket of fried chicken?" he asked the instant I walked into his room.

"This is not your last meal," I snapped.

"We don't know that do we?"

"Murder Dub and hang, you want that last meal so bad."

"Where's my chicken?"

"They ran out," I answered. "All they had was macaroni and cheese."

"I hate macaroni and cheese."

"That's why I didn't bring you any. So, why'd you shoot Dub?"

"I got inspired. I saw this t-shirt that showed an old guy - a barbed wire tough old bastard - leaning back against a vintage Hog 1200 with a "don't even think it" expression and the caption, *"Don't mess with this old man. A life sentence don't mean squat to me.""*

"So, you shot him."

"He was wearing canvas trousers, turned his back, bent over, and wiggled his ass at me, so I sprinkled him."

"Any reason?"

"Never been but one."

"And that is?"

"You know that bastard called me a traitor?"

"Why's that? Because your rabbi is gay?"

"Being a prick is one thing. You don't want people walking on your lawn? Fine. You don't want people talking in the movie? Fine. You're worshiping Elvis? Be my guest. You're not asking me to like you. You're asking me to mind my own business. Fine. But do not get in my face like the scum sucking pig you are with your degenerate Nazi conspiracy crap. Fuckin' bottom feeder." Poppa couldn't stop himself. The nurse ordered a drip.

"Fly a confederate flag and you've got the 'nads to tell me I'm the traitor? You tell the United States of America to fuck off so you can steal people and work them 'til they die, and I'm the traitor? Go pack sand, Mussolini!"

This diatribe did not sit well with the medical staff, nor did the ones that followed. Nobody said he was deranged, but he could not stop raving, which sent his blood pressure into the stratosphere. They wanted him to calm down before they released him. He wouldn't.

"And get this American factoid. Slave owners took out life insurance policies on their slaves. Slave drops dead. Send the check."

"Finished?" I asked.

"For now."

I assured the shrinks he'd be fine at home with me. They asked me to give them a couple of days, so, of course, I said sure.

"Before you leave, take the dagger out of my back," he said.

"Do it yourself," I assured him.

"Can I get a beer with that fried chicken?"

"No alcohol," warned the head nurse.

"I use the crapper by myself," he stated.

"If you do, we'll tie you down," she said.

"Try it."

`Bottom line: Poppa grew a bit more belligerent by the day. *Mendacity* was his favorite word. Tucker Carlson and Rachel Maddow were forbidden. Might as well deprive this man of oxygen.

"Why don't you cut my wrists?" he yelled.

"I'd get too much blood on my scrubs," his nurse retorted.

"Whatever happened to compassion?" he asked.

"You wear me out. Ring the bell if you want me," she said heading for the door.

"Suppose I don't want you?"

"Your loss," she said.

*

I never expected he would die, at least, not when he did, probably not forever, probably not at all. Would I ever have been? Prepared for it? Poppa was so angry they were reluctant to release him.

"They want me to calm down," he told me. "*Make good trouble.* Who said that?"

"John Lewis."

"You know about my relationship with Angela Davis?", he asked.

"Tell me."

"I told you."

"Tell me again."

"Very nice smile."

He paused and took a deep breath.

Kiddo," he said to me, "Take me home."

*

"'*Take small steps 'n' take 'em slow. If you can step on it, step over it. If you can step over it, step around it. That way you'll live to climb more mountains.'* Fellow that I worked with from the Ozarks told me that's how his daddy taught him to climb mountains."

"What's your point?" I asked.

"Pass it on," he said. "It's a wisdom."

Poppa'd been home a week or so, took his meds like a trooper, worked on his family grove, keeping mostly to himself. He chafed about not being allowed to drive, but one day I looked and the truck was gone. So was Reuben Henry. He came back two hours later with a truck bed filled with butterfly bush, two dogwoods, firebush, and two lapin cherry trees. Poppa bitched about his loss of stamina, but his strength was intact and his determination never left. His grove became a spot for thinking, for taking a nap, for snacking on sweet, fresh apples and crisp pears - misshapen but pearl drop tasty - for basking in fruited air. A cloister must be like this. Where Moses saw a bush that burned, Poppa saw a bush that shone and bore fruit and gave shade and grew more. Their wedding oak was now an old tree with a hollow at its base where a dwarf might take shelter. Poppa had kept Sophie Rose's ashes in a black walnut box he'd made himself with a small latch crafted from a sliver of antler and a rawhide lace. I went out one day and saw the box in the hollow at the base of that tree. Poppa hadn't said a word about it.

"I want you to have what we had, only a lot longer. If we could've bottled that smile of hers, we'd be rich as Rockefeller. Funny. Off the wall funny. Big thing I always liked about being in the country is that a man can go outside to take a whiz."

"Thank you for sharing, but what's that got to do with grandma?"

"We were living in Montana when I stepped outside under an apple tree to tap my bladder. I was singing ``*Well, before I'll be a slave, I'll be buried in my grave...*'' when this white-faced hornet buried his stinger in the head of my pride 'n' joy. My Moses. He parted the Red Sea. The pain was excruciating, I mean, branding iron excruciating. Sophie Rose heard me screaming and ran outside to see what was wrong. She couldn't stop laughing. Thanks a lot, Soph."

"I'm really sorry about the pain," she said, but the swelling was terrific."

"I'm not sure I needed to hear that," I said.

"Sophie Rose was the best. You saw where she is, yes?"

"Yes."

"OK, then," he said.

*

One morning he wanted to know where was Buster?

"Chasing rabbits," I said.

"Good dog, old Buster," he noted with great respect.

*

Last night Poppa dreamt I was in danger. Three giant men on stilts with long black greatcoats skirting the ground were hovering over me, about to swoop down like vultures. Poppa took off running, leapt on their backs, slammed their heads together...and broke a rib when he hit the floor. Jumped out of bed. Screaming.

"Like a spear going through me," he said.

Nothing to do about a broken rib. Tough it out. Try not to cough. Hug yourself hard. Soldier on. Percodan every four to six hours. Percocet? Phooey.

Hit his head, too. Thick carpet. Good thing. Once again, worth the price, that carpet, Poppa said. I did notice his balance was a bit off, his memory not quite as keen. Being older, stuff happens. The problem with stuff happening at his age is that stuff keeps happening at his age.

*

He came in one day and said he'd been showing Crockett around the place. Crockett? West Virginia? That Crockett?

"I've been wanting him to see where I shot my last deer."

"Wait a minute" I said. "Crockett from West Virginia? Here?"

"You know any other Crockett?"

"I'm still waiting to meet this one."

"He'd appreciate this. Listen up."

"Excuse me?"

"I was sitting against a tree at the top of that hill looking down at the creek. I was late getting up there that morning, so I didn't have any great expectations, just thought I'd take a look. I sat back and took in the morning which was not just any morning but a morning in hunting season. Deer had already been moving for hours, ever since the first hunter entered the woods. The scent of well-oiled guns puts them on the alert. Your blood runs on cue. A good deer would fill the freezer for months, an elk for a year. Whisper. To myself? "Where's my deer?" Out there somewhere. I closed my eyes and thought of him. I saw him in a clearing, a young buck, a fork horn with three older ones. Those elders stayed alert, while the young forky kept his nose to the ground. Let theirs be in the wind."

"I watched him wander off wondering where next? What next? Why next? If I were him...He...I emptied my mind of everything but that one manifest deer. I could still see him clearly. I saw that deer! The way I'm seeing you. That's the way I saw him. He was on the move. Nothing else existed on earth except me and him. Just the two of us. We were bound. I knew it, and he was drawn by it. Time was nothing. I did not let him out of my sight. I did not move. My eyes stayed put. And right then and there I heard him. At first, I thought the hoofbeats came from a horse that got loose, but it was lighter than a horse, a daintier sound, brushed against my sleeve, dirt kicked up. I looked up. He jumped the creek, stopped on the other side, and looked back. Only for a second. Long enough."

Chapter 16

The Championship Rounds

Poppa told me, "In boxing there exists a solitary zone of time known as "The Championship Rounds", the final two, the time in a fight when the fighter must dig as deeply as ever to keep fighting with all his heart and soul, must dig in more than he ever imagined he could, than he ever imagined was even possible in this world. No matter how hurt, how tired, how exhausted, how much your arms ache to drop by your sides, how unable you are to keep slipping punches, how unable you are to do anything but fight back with all the ferocity you suffered to acquire – fight the urge to surrender, no desire to do anything but keep on until it's stopped by the bell or the punch you don't see. His goal is to dig in and stay alive. He does not break. He pushes himself with all his heart because that's where it's at, the heart, that's where it comes from, the heart. The will can give out, but not the heart, never the heart."

"The situation is crystal clear. Just the two of you. Three straight minutes - a blink in time; a millennium in the ring - where the other guy's singular mission is to destroy you. This is not a negotiation. No compromise is possible. Or sought. You are alone. Nobody at your side. Nobody at your back. No time out. No shrieking whistle terminating the play. You have been cut loose. You are free. All choices gone but one. We cross the boundary into pure survival. There is no thought of death, and there is liberation in that."

*

I wouldn't call Poppa a sports fanatic. He liked a good game from time to time, almost any game, except for that Canadian thing with brooms and golf, specifically, golf on TV. Follow the bouncing ball. He hated it. His passion was boxing. Even as a little girl he was teaching me the "old one-two".

That friend of mine - I mentioned him, right? - That doc I worked with in Zimbabwe? - He made one really smart move when he bought us all ringside seats to a championship fight at Madison Square Garden. Men attired in smart suits with big rings on rough fingers actually came over to shake Poppa's hand. The one or two times my friend visited, he and Poppa spent the entire time watching videos of classic prize fights. Sugar Ray Robinson and Jake LaMotta? How 'bout that one? 'Ray, I'm still standing. I'm still standing, Ray,' said Jake LaMotta to Sugar Ray Robinson when the bell rang to end fifteen. He'd been badly whipped, was hanging against the ropes but still on his feet. Never went down. Shakespeare? Keats? Frederick Douglas? Winston Churchill? Forget them. LaMotta's remained Poppa's favorite quote of all time. 'I'm still standing, Ray. Ray, I'm still standing.'

*

You don't go to a gym to look pretty and drink flavored water. You don't go to a gym to flirt, at least, not this one, not unless you want to be carried out by first responders. Beat up punching bags swing by rusty chains from the ceiling. Old steel army surplus lockers with dents and scratches. Folding chairs. Two rings filled with ghosts. Nobody's there for fancy. Still, you see more six packs at a boxing gym than your local bodega, only a boxer's six are developed to withstand a depth charge. Imposing as a wrought iron gate, they signal danger. Yet, nobody's strutting, posturing, acting tough, bragging. Outside, maybe, too many beers, maybe, but not in the gym. These guys train to fight and survive in a very tough trade. Punch after punch after punch until muscle memory is fixed in place. Three minutes. One round. It will never end. He's right in front of me. Why can't I touch him?

Poppa put on an amazing performance for an old man as he bobbed and weaved and shadow boxed around the living room, throwing combinations, right cross, uppercut, hook off the jab. "Controlling the center of the ring, baby. Controlling the center of the ring."

"I loved the sounds of the place. Another world, Thea. Time in beats of 3's and 1's, the thud of mitts, the speed bag ratatata, the whump whap whump of the heavy bag, grunts and shuffles, leather ropes slapping the floor with skippy rhythm, the three-minute bell, the one-minute bell. Get this, Thea. You're not gonna believe this one."

"Try me."

"Jack Dempsey actually hummed as he came forward!"

*

"There are three minutes from my life that I value more than most," he told me.

"Freddie Brown, Roberto Duran's trainer and cut man, trained me at the venerable Gleason's Gym. Freddie was a tough old bird, an ex-fighter himself with a career that left his nose on the wrong side of his face. Freddie was a banger. He stood there and fought it out. I don't know that Freddie was ever knocked off his feet. I do know that every three minutes he was in there he'd fight as if they were his last, 'cause that's what y'do."

"Freddie wore the same old threadbare cardigan daily with a pocketful of hard candy. "Fighters are like racehorses," he told me, "They do something good, you give 'em a piece of candy."

"Kill the body, and the head will follow" was another truism. "Punches in bunches" was a good one, too. But the best? "Don't think about what he's gonna do to you. Think about what you're gonna do to him."

"So, one day Freddie agrees to a match-up between me and a guy 15 years younger than me prepping for a professional fight. I was not a pro, just a gym rat with a so-so jab who happened to like hanging around boxers. This kid's face, I swear - eyes like pock marks - displayed all the tenderness of a death camp guard. OK. Let's do this. Bell rings. Guy rips from his corner, immediately clips me point blank on the chin, sending me flying backwards, off-balance. "Don't fall," I kept saying to myself. "Don't fall. Just get to those ropes, balance, bounce back." Do it! An act of will. I stayed on my feet, hit the ropes, balanced myself, sling shot back out there. It was raw survival. Adolph comes at me. This was it. He's doing his Joe Frazier – hunched low, bobbing, weaving, coming forward, both hands cutting loose. Get killed, or…I began firing jabs at him, jab after jab, jab after jab – bam, bam, bam – Keep him away. Don't let him get close."

"Feint left. Fake right. Duck under his jab! Jab. Jab. Jab. If he gets close, he'll kill me. Jab! Jab! Double up. Low. High. Bam. Bam. BamBam. What right hand? Just keep jabbing. Bell rings. I'm still standing. He looks disgusted. Tough. I walk back to my corner. Freddie had a piece of candy ready for me."

I screamed and cheered Poppa on like a teen-ager. Way to go, Champ. Money's on you! Way to go!" I clapped my hands so hard my palms went red.

"Now that I know for certain that the welterweight belt is out of reach, I can sleep. It's all about the Championship Rounds, Thea. Maybe it gets to be golden somewhere down the line, maybe, but I don't see sitting back and waiting. Can you make it to the end with what you've got, or can you still do better? The knockout punch is the one you never see. I'm walkin' along, singin' my song, just drop me in my tracks. No regrets. Just trying to wrap this old, battered brain around it all. Remember when I joked about burying me in my Marine Corps uniform in case I have to fight my way out of Hell? There is a Hell, Thea, but not what you think."

"No imps with forked tongues and pitchforks?"

"Worse. You're dying. You know you're dying. You know you are seconds away from one last breath. How do you want those final mites of time to be? Anxious because you didn't pay the electric bill? Hey, the lights are going out, anyway, so? Graceful? Peaceful? Of course. But suppose your last thoughts are bitter, resentful, churning with malice, downright murderous. The torture of a thousand cuts fills your heart with joy. You haven't killed somebody you still hate and wish you had. You haven't torn them to shreds. But you still want to, and, God willing, you still and forever will. You die with those wretched thoughts intact as long as consciousness lasts, so, for all intents and purposes, that's your forever, that's your Eternity, and you're locked into it. Me? Peace 'n' Love, Toots. Peace 'n' Love. No surrender. Wish me luck."

"Good luck, Champ," I said, flashing him the V for Victory.

"Stay tuned," he said. "Thea, I truly thought once I got this far, I'd have a few answers. Life is exhilarating. Life is humbling. A little forgiveness never hurt. Other than that, my thoughts are twisters. I do wonder, if not for grief, would we be here forever?"

"Walk the earth without it?" I asked.

"I will not miss the milkweeds and the monarchs and the red oak or the wild thyme, but I will miss you and that's where the grief comes in. Life is not just human, y'know. Human's die but life does not. It lives. It goes on. It grows. It changes. It stays. Did it start from something? Does it matter? It's here."

He puts his arm around me. "Like you 'n' me, Toots."

"Are you planning on going somewhere?"

"Not that I know of."

When the time did come, he was like an old dog who wandered off into the bush. It was way before light when I heard the door open and shut. Nothing unusual since Poppa often went out into the dark. He loved transitions - dark to light to dark. "My morning rush," he'd explain. "Keep your coffee. Better yet, keep it hot. Later, Toots."

I found him resting against the old oak tree holding a carefully lettered sign:

Sorry to miss the fried chicken. I love you madly.

No sign of pain, no sign of discomfort, resting, with something of his smile.

There was a note in Poppa's pocket.

Don't worry. Nothing hurts. This was not my doing. I came up here to rest. Life has been grand. I wouldn't mind a little bit more, but what the hell. 'Know when to hold 'em. Know when to fold 'em.' I always liked Kenny Rogers. Stay strong, Toots. Water my tree. Lavender would be my next choice. A ring of lavender surrounding the grove. Africans call it a "boma". Just make certain there's enough drainage.

I will not miss the creek after the rain, moonlight shadows, salamanders, dew on bare toes, or wild violets, but I will miss you. I'm reconciled to the fact that I've had my place and performed according to plan and I accept what every wild animal and sentient plant accepts: where I've been, what I've been, will become something else. I am not finished here.

*

My friend came to Poppa's funeral. He asked me to marry him. I said *only if we can live here*. He said, yes. *And raise our children here*. Yes.

*

We placed Poppa's ashes next to Sophie Rose's in the hollow of their tree. There would be no stone, but the local obit published his picture with bunting around it and proclaimed in full, fat, deep black letters:

"Been a Bad Ol' Booger but He's Come 'n' Gone."

ACKNOWLEDGMENTS

Without the guidance of Tracy Haught, my editor, *HOME* might have been a hodgepodge of scenes and not a coherent narrative. Thank you, Tracy.

Without the love and support from all of you, the struggle would be that much harder. Time is short, and I am grateful: Dyanne Asimow, Eric Rickstad, Alan Winter, Joel Edward Foreman, Ellen "Elfnarts" Sack, Jon Scieszka, Casey Scieszka, Thom Mount, Gene Seymour, David Rosenthal, Brooke Adams, Lynne Adams Fifield, Tony Shalhoub, Jerome Gary, Reuben Hermanson Sack, Jon Foreman, Alex Schub and Eleanor Bigolsky, Judith Ren-Lay, Steve Adams, Roger Hendricks Simon, Jules Older, Carol Jaspin, Rashid Miller, Bill Murray, June Omura Wheeler, Bob Getz, Jenny Allen, and Larry Block aka The Blumster.

And for so many days and nights, months and years, myriad moments of joy and happiness, there has been my family, my wife and partner, Jamie Donnelly, and my two children, Sevi D and Madden Rose, my gemstones, my gifts, my blessings. Without you there would be no words at all.